**He wasn't going to let her leave the life she had made for herself because some bully of a man had it in his mind that he could come here and hurt her.**

"I won't let him hurt you. You know that."

"I knew you'd say that. That's why I didn't want to tell you. I don't want to get you involved in this," Jo said before turning her back to him. He watched as her arms came around her body as if to hold herself together.

Unable to stop himself, he went to her and put his arms around her, pulling her back against him. "I'm already involved. We're a team. You know that. Alex and Summer, they'll feel the same way once we tell them what's going on. None of us are going to sit around and let this guy bully you."

She pulled away from him and he let her go, though he wanted to keep her close to him, where he knew she would be safe.

Dear Reader,

Everyone who knows me knows that I am a big supporter of all nurses. Of all the things I've done in my life, besides being a mother, I am most proud of my career as a nurse. This month marks the thirty-year anniversary of the first day I walked into the hospital as a nurse. You cannot imagine how scared I was that day. Being responsible for someone else's care can be frightening, but every day millions of nurses show up and do the job. I'm proud to say that both one of my daughters and one of my sons are among that number.

As we celebrate International Nurses Day this month, my hope is that everyone can look back and have a memory of at least one nurse who went that extra step and showed them the compassion and care that Florence Nightingale envisioned.

I also hope that you will enjoy Jo and Casey's story as they work to care for the citizens of Key West while finding the love that these two best friends have been denying for years. I found their commitment to their patients and to each other was inspiring, and I hope you do, too.

Best wishes,

*Deanne*

# FLIGHT NURSE'S FLORIDA FAIRY TALE

———

## DEANNE ANDERS

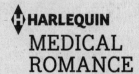

**HARLEQUIN**
MEDICAL
ROMANCE

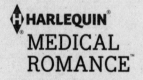

# HARLEQUIN®
# MEDICAL ROMANCE™

Recycling programs for this product may not exist in your area.

ISBN-13: 978-1-335-73785-4

Flight Nurse's Florida Fairy Tale

For questions and comments about the quality of this book, please contact us at CustomerService@Harlequin.com.

Harlequin Enterprises ULC
22 Adelaide St. West, 41st Floor
Toronto, Ontario M5H 4E3, Canada
www.Harlequin.com

**Printed in U.S.A.**

**Deanne Anders** was reading romance while her friends were still reading Nancy Drew, and she knew she'd hit the jackpot when she found a shelf of Harlequin Presents in her local library. Years later she discovered the fun of writing her own. Deanne lives in Florida with her husband and their spoiled Pomeranian. During the day she works as a nursing supervisor. With her love of everything medical and romance, writing for Harlequin Medical Romance is a dream come true.

### Books by Deanne Anders

### Harlequin Medical Romance

Visit the Author Profile page at Harlequin.com.

For all the first responders in Florida,
Cuba and South Carolina for their work in the
aftermath of Hurricane Ian

# CHAPTER ONE

"WHAT HAVE YOU DONE?"

Casey Johnson looked up from the crossword puzzle he had been working on for the last thirty minutes. He should have left work an hour ago, but he just didn't have the energy or the desire to face his empty house this morning. It was funny how watching someone fight for their life made you look at your own in a different light.

A pretty blonde stood above him, her face flushed red, with one baby on her hip and another in some type of sling across her chest. He searched his mind for what he could have done that would have set off Summer, his coworker and his boss's wife. The only thing he'd done in the last fourteen hours was work. Had he done something wrong on duty? Had someone complained about something he'd said or done?

The last call they'd responded to had been a rough one and the reason he had gotten himself engrossed in the daily crossword challenge. It was his way of escaping from all the horrific scenes that were sometimes part of the job. But this last call, a head-on collision, had been particularly hard to deal with. He pictured the small child they'd flown to the children's hospital in Miami. He had fought the urge to call and check on her condition ever since they had arrived back at headquarters. But sometimes not knowing was for the best. Otherwise this job could destroy you. You did everything possible for your patient, and then you had to walk away.

No, there was nothing that anyone could have been upset about on that call last night. He'd done everything in his power to keep their tiny patient alive. He just hoped it had been enough.

"Well, what did you do?" Summer's voice had lost some of its demand, but it still had a bite to it that he didn't understand.

"Maybe you could give me a hint?" Casey said as he laid down the daily paper, all interest in it gone now that he was remembering the last call of his shift. It was better to deal with Summer and whatever it was that had gotten her upset at him than to think about the patient he'd left clinging to life.

"Uh, Jo, of course." Summer juggled the baby from one hip to the other without taking her scorching glare from him.

"What about her? All I did was cover for her last night, just like she asked. It isn't like it was my fault that she got sick. It was probably that five-alarm salsa she ate at that new cantina we went to yesterday. I warned her that it would burn a hole in her stomach."

"She didn't tell you?" Summer asked, then turned away from him. "Of course she didn't. If she had, you would have talked her out of it." It was as if Summer deflated in front of him as she sunk into the chair beside him while repositioning the babies in her lap.

"Tell me what?" Whatever had Summer this upset couldn't be good. But why did she think it was something he had done? It wasn't his fault Jo was so sick that she couldn't work her shift.

"Jo called this morning and turned in her resignation. She's leaving the island," a voice said from behind him.

He watched as his boss, Alex Leonelli,

aka Prince Alexandros of Soura, stepped around him, bent down to kiss his wife and then each of his children. Casey was happy that his two coworkers had finally managed to patch things up, but there was something about that secret look that passed between them that sent a jolt of jealousy through him.

Not that he was truly jealous. He didn't need all the drama that came along with a serious relationship. He was happy with his life as it was. He had a job he loved and friends, like Jo Kemp, who he could always count on.

It hit him then what Alex had said. Jo had turned in her resignation? No. That was impossible. It hadn't been twenty-four hours since he'd last seen her. They were best friends. There was no way she would do something like that without talking to him about it first. Besides, she loved her job as flight nurse for the Key West office of Heli-Care. She'd never quit.

"Is this some kind of joke?" he asked them. "Are you two punking me?"

"Of course not," Summer said. And from the sag of her shoulders and the miserable look in her eyes, he had no choice but to believe her.

"There has to be a mistake." He'd been surprised when Jo had called to say she couldn't make her shift. She'd seemed fine earlier in the day, but there had been no missing the anxiety in her voice. He'd assumed she was worried about finding someone to cover her shift, though now that he thought about it, her voice had still seemed strained after he had reassured her that he could cover for her. So what had happened?

"She had to have given you a reason," Casey said as he stood, turning toward Alex.

"She said it was personal." Alex bent and took one of the twins from his wife.

"I tried to call her," Summer said as Casey pulled his phone from his pocket, "but she's not answering."

"Maybe she's still sleeping." Casey looked at the time on his phone, surprised when he saw that it was after eight in the morning already. "I'll just stop by on my way home and see if I can get to the bottom of this."

"I'm not sure that's a good idea," Summer said, grabbing hold of his arm as he went to pick up the duffel bag he'd dropped earlier. "Maybe you should wait until she tells you herself."

Casey patted her hand before pulling his arm away and taking his sunglasses out of his shirt pocket. "I don't think so. I know Jo. She loves her job. Something has to be wrong, and I'm going to find out what it is."

He'd heard it in her voice last night. She'd been breathless and very anxious to get off the phone. He'd assumed it was because she wasn't feeling well, but now he wasn't sure. Had she just been afraid to tell him that she was leaving?

He headed to the door. He and Jo had started at Heli-Care the same day over four years ago. He'd come to the company after flying search and rescue for the coast guard and then obtaining his nurse's license, while she had been an experienced nurse on her first flight assignment. They'd become the best of friends, and the Jo he knew wasn't afraid of anything. Especially not him.

"Casey, please tell her to call me," Summer called from behind him.

He waved back at her, acknowledging her request. By the time he finished talking with Jo and fixing whatever the problem she had, the only call she'd have to make was the one telling Alex that she had changed her mind.

There was no way he was going to let Jo quit her job. And there was no way he was going to let her leave him behind. And if she didn't stay?

Choosing to ignore that thought, he blamed the sudden gnawing pain in his stomach on his last shift. He wasn't worried. Jo had been fine the day before. Whatever had happened since they'd had lunch together yesterday could be fixed. It was the fact that she hadn't told him about any of this that bothered him the most.

What could be so bad that she couldn't tell him? He'd thought they had a special friendship. One where she would be able to tell him anything. That she couldn't trust him to help her, that was the real problem. Because if she didn't trust him enough to talk to him before she did something as drastic as quitting her job and leaving town, how could he help her?

Jo sat on the floor and rubbed Moose's head. Her Great Dane had known something was wrong the moment she'd gotten off the phone, and he had spent the night trying to comfort her. Finally, unable to sleep, she'd gotten up and started the job of packing. Again.

For four years she'd stayed hidden. Four glorious years of feeling safe. She should have known it couldn't last. Nothing ever did.

"Well, Moose, we can sit here and bemoan our future, or we can start working. What will it be?" The dog's large tongue shot out and licked her from collarbone to cheek in one swipe. "Yeah, I don't want to do it either, but we don't really have a choice."

She'd spent the night going over all her options, and the only one that made sense was for her to get out of town as soon as possible. The last thing she wanted was to drag her friends into her problems. As her parents' had reminded her, she'd created the problem and it was her job to take care of it. Though as her sister had said, running away was not really taking care of anything. And then there was her brother offering to take care of the problem for her, something that would have had him spending time in jail instead of in college where he belonged. Thank goodness the courts had dealt with Jeffrey before her brother had gotten his chance.

The knock on the door startled her. Instinct had her hand going for Moose's collar while she looked around the apartment for a weapon of any sort.

The knock came again, but this time it was followed by a voice both she and Moose recognized. "Jo, open the door."

Moose pulled out of her hold, reminding her that she only remained in control of the big dog because he chose to let her. Standing, she looked down at the corner where she had been huddled then raised her hand, which held a spatula. How had that gotten there? She laid it on the kitchen counter and followed her dog to the door. A part of her, the scared part, wanted nothing more than to throw herself into Casey's big arms where she knew she would be safe from whatever it was her ex had planned for her.

Another part, the sane part, knew that would be a mistake. The last thing she needed was to let Casey know that something, or someone, had scared her. If she was lucky, he had just stopped by to check and see if she was getting over being "sick" the night before. She'd hated having to lie to him, but the alternative wasn't something that she could share. Eventually she'd have to tell him her plans, not that she had formed any, but for now Casey didn't know that she had turned in her resignation.

"Hold on a moment," she called as she tried to pull Moose away from the door so she could open it. Once the door was opened and all six feet five inches of the man she considered her best friend stood in front of her, she truly realized just how hard leaving her home and her friends was going to be. How was she supposed to walk away from here? How could she leave someone like Casey who had become so important in her life?

Her hands shook as she let go of Moose and he launched himself into Casey's arms. The dog had a special friendship with the man, just like she did. There had been a time when she'd hoped that she and Casey could be more than friends, but she'd accepted long ago that that was all Casey wanted from her. And it worked. They worked. If she occasionally suffered from a stray dream that had them participating in more romantic activities, what did it hurt? They were her secret, and something that she would never have to share with him.

And just because she still felt that little zing of pleasure that was far from friendly whenever he threw his arm around her or that painful sting of envy whenever he brought his latest girlfriend around, that wasn't a good enough reason to risk losing him and their friendship.

Though now it looked like she would be losing it anyway. Maybe she should have taken a chance for more when her friend Summer had suggested it a few months ago after Casey had broken up with his fifth girlfriend in as many months.

But none of that mattered anymore. Right now, all that mattered was that she keep him from seeing the fear that had her heart pounding with a tachycardic rhythm that it couldn't maintain if she wanted to keep standing.

"What are you doing here?" she asked as she held on to the door, hoping to stabilize her trembling hands as well as use it to help hold her up.

The look in his green eyes and the arch of one blond eyebrow told her all she needed to know. Had it been too much to hope Alex would keep the news of her resignation for at least a few hours?

She started to tell him that she was still feeling ill and he shouldn't be around her. It wasn't really a lie. She'd definitely felt better. But one look at Casey's stubborn squared-off jaw told her he wasn't going to leave until they talked.

"Come on in," she said as she opened the door. Now that her body was getting over its fight or flight instinct, she knew it was for the best to get this over with. Better to deal with him now than let the anticipation of telling him goodbye keep her tied up in knots.

Her apartment was small, a little living room, dining room and kitchen combination, with one small bedroom and bathroom in the back. When Casey walked in, it seemed to shrink even more. His head was just inches from touching the ceiling, and his shoulders barely fit through the small opening between the dining room and kitchen.

The size of him had intimidated her when she'd first met him, but within days she knew that she could trust this man to never hurt her. He didn't have a violent bone in his body.

"So it's true. You're leaving," he said as he stared down at the pile of pots and pans she had pulled out of the cabinets to pack.

"You spoke to Alex," she said. Not an answer really, but it was all she had. Admitting that she was leaving was too hard.

"You know I spoke to Alex. And when he told me that you had resigned, I told him he had to be mistaken. You'd never leave a job that you loved or a crew that is as much family as coworkers. And to do it without giving any notice? I knew he had to be mistaken." His eyes, those sweet, light green eyes that were usually filled with warmth and humor had gone hard now. "Do you know why I told him he had to be mistaken?"

She shook her head. His voice, usually booming, had gone quiet. He was angry. Very angry. At her.

And even though he was almost twice the size of Jeffrey, her ex-husband, his anger didn't scare her. She'd seen this man intubate the smallest of infants, his big hands gentle in their touch. She'd watched him carry a fragile elderly woman, who'd fallen and broken her hip, all the while reassuring her with his calming voice. She knew Casey. Knew him better than she had ever known her ex-husband. Even when he was as angry as he was at her right now, she knew she was safe.

And it wasn't just her heart that told her

this. It was her body. It didn't tremble as Casey glared at her. Her eyes didn't dart around the room looking for a place to hide. She was safe with him. He was someone she could trust. Someone she could share her fear with and know that he wouldn't judge her because of the mistakes she'd made years ago.

So why hadn't she told him about her past before now? Pride? Embarrassment? Both? Her marriage had ended more than five years ago, and she still felt stupid for falling for her ex's lies.

And then there was the shame. While she knew she had been an innocent victim, she still felt shame when she thought of how she'd let her husband break her. She'd let her fear of him imprison her, freezing her in place, until she had lost the ability and the will to fight back.

Did she admit all this to Casey now? Would he still respect her when he discovered she wasn't the badass nurse he thought her to be? She guessed she'd soon find out.

"No, why?" she asked, knowing he needed to tell her, even though she already knew the answer.

"Because I knew that you would never have

done something like that without talking to me, telling me first," Casey said. He'd begun to pace the six-foot path from the kitchen to her living room, making it necessary for him to turn every couple steps. She started to laugh at the sight, but she knew he wouldn't appreciate it.

"I can explain," she started, and then recognized the words as ones she used to use with Jeffrey. Why did she have to explain herself? She'd called Alex because her first responsibility was to her boss and the company she worked for. She was going to be leaving them short-staffed, and that was something she would never have done if she'd had a choice. But still, it had hurt Casey that she hadn't told him first and she couldn't help but feel bad about it.

She straightened her shoulders and began again. "I'm sorry I didn't notify you of my decision. I was going to call you later today after you'd gotten some sleep."

"What? On your way out of town?" he asked.

She didn't answer him. His words were too close to the truth.

"I just don't get it," Casey said. He stopped

pacing and took a seat on the leather love seat she'd saved for months to buy. She'd decided sometime during the night that she could only take what she could load in her car. She'd have to leave it behind, just like the life she'd made here. She was leaving almost everything. Including a piece of her heart that she wasn't certain she could ever get back.

Casey ran his hands through his blond curls, which always seemed to be in the need of a trimming. "Just tell me why. Why have you suddenly decided that you need to leave? It can't be the job. You love your job."

"I do love my job," Jo said, taking a seat next to him.

"I know it's not the island, you love the Keys. Has someone made you a better offer?"

"No. Of course it's not another job. I wouldn't do that to Alex." There wasn't another job out there that would be good enough to make her leave the island and her friends.

"Is it me?" Casey asked. "Did I do something?"

"What?" His question startled her. "Why would you think it was something you had done?"

"Maybe because Summer thinks it's because of me," he said. He turned toward her, his eyes questioning her.

"Well, Summer is wrong. It has nothing to do with you," she said.

She'd known she should never have admitted her attraction to Casey to Summer. They'd been at a party. It had been late. She'd worked the night before, and they'd responded to a multicar pileup that had stayed with her long after they'd flown the last victim to a Miami trauma center. Both she and Casey had known that the young man wasn't going to survive. She'd been in a gloomy mood as she wrestled with the age-old question of why life wasn't fair. Then she'd seen Casey leave the party with another woman. Before she knew what she was doing, she'd spilled everything that she thought was wrong with the woman to Summer and why she, Jo, should have been the woman leaving with him.

It was the next morning, when she realized what she had done, that she made the decision to put whatever feelings she had for Casey behind her. She wasn't going to be that bitter woman who wasted her time over a man who wasn't interested in her that way. Since then, no matter how much Summer had tried to get her to tell Casey how she felt, she'd refused. She had to accept their friendship for what it was. And she was glad that she had. No matter that sometimes she found herself shooting invisible arrows at the women he dated, she was happy with their relationship as it stood. She had to be.

"I'll never understand women," Casey said. His hand reached out and covered hers, but the intimacy of the act was lost on him. To him, she was just a best friend he was comfortable touching. To her, his touch reminded her of things she would never experience with him. Things that would have her blushing if he could read her mind.

"No, you never will," she said, shaking her head then laughing. "And that's probably a good thing."

"What?" he asked, before shaking his own head. "Never mind. Forget about Summer. Tell me what's wrong."

Pulling her hand from under his, she turned toward him. Did she tell him the truth? That the reason she'd moved to Key West in the first place had been because she was running away from her abusive ex-husband? Did she tell him that now she had to run again?

She didn't believe Casey had ever been afraid of anything. He'd told stories about his time in the coast guard that made her shiver with the knowledge of how close he had come to being killed each and every time they'd conducted a raid on a drug cartel's boat. How could she expect someone like him, someone who knew no fear, to understand the terror that filled her every time she thought of her ex finding her?

# CHAPTER TWO

CASEY WAS TRYING his best to be patient. He'd seen how shaken Jo was when he'd arrived and had immediately known there was something very wrong. The fact that she hadn't denied that she was leaving the island made it even more evident that something had changed between the time they had left the cantina the day before and the time she had called him to cover her shift. But what?

"Is it a man?" He didn't know what made him ask the question. Maybe it was the memory of Anna leaving town all those years ago. She'd left a note stating she met someone that she truly loved. That it was the night before their wedding had just been one more turn of the knife in his heart. Could it be that Jo had met someone who'd talked her into leaving with him, too?

The silence that followed his question was

all the answer he needed. He could put up a fight against Jo for leaving because of a new job or if someone had done something to upset her. He could fix that. But another man? Just the thought of Jo with another man threatened the control he had on his anger, though he knew he had no right to those feelings. They were best friends. He couldn't and wouldn't cross that line even if it left him frustrated at the moment. And besides these crazy proprietary feelings he was having, he had no weapons to use if she had fallen for some man, even if he knew right away that he couldn't be worthy of his Jo.

But she wasn't his. Not that way. There was no way to win this fight.

"So do you love him?" he asked.

"Love him?" Jo asked, her voice hoarse and her eyes wide as she looked up at him. "No, I don't think I ever did really. And that's on me. A lot of this is on me."

Her hands seemed to tremble as she ran them across her face, rubbing at her eyes that were red and swollen. Maybe she had been sick the night before. But still, her answer didn't make any sense. If she didn't love this man, why was she leaving with him? None of this made sense.

"Just tell me what's going on, Jo. Whatever it is, I can help."

He waited as she took a deep breath then looked him in the eyes. Was it possible that their chocolate brown color was even darker? Or was it just the haunted, desperate look she gave him?

"I don't know where to start. It all seems so ridiculous, so crazy. Like one of those made for TV movies that come on in the afternoon. But it's real. Do you know what I mean? It's like when we see some of those accidents our patients get themselves into and we say that we couldn't make this stuff up."

He just nodded. He had her talking now, and he didn't want to interrupt her. If she was in some type of trouble, they'd find a way to fix it.

"I met Jeffrey at a company party that was for my father's retirement. They were both partners in the same law firm, and my father thought a lot of him. My father said he went at a case like a dog after a bone. I didn't realize then that I would become the bone in that analogy." Jo looked around the room, and her lips turned down as they began to tremble. "I thought it was over. All of it. I thought I would be safe here."

"You are safe. I'll keep you safe. I promise," Casey said. If it was this ex she was afraid of, he would make it a point to have a talk with the man.

Jo suddenly stood. "How about I make us some lemonade? I have a bunch of lemons I can't take with me."

"That sounds good," Casey said, though his stomach had become a churning acid filled pit since he'd learned of Jo's leaving. And now? Now, he just wanted to punch something after seeing how scared she was.

He followed her into the small kitchen and found the pitcher sitting in a pile of dishes on the cabinet. It appeared that she had been sorting things to pack as there was another pile on the floor in a corner.

They worked together quietly, as they did when they worked flights together, neither one of them having to tell the other what they needed to do next. Once the lemons had been squeezed and the ice, sugar and cold water had been added, Jo poured them both tall glasses of the tart drink. Thinking a change in setting might be nice, he picked up the glasses and took them out to the patio off the back of her apartment, setting them on a small table.

"Tell me everything," Casey said, as they each took a seat facing the flower garden Jo had planted.

Her eyes met his and then dropped. "I was so dumb. There were flags, bright red flags waving in front of my face that I should have seen. I let myself be blinded by Jeffrey's charm. I was such a fool."

"I know you, Jo. You're not dumb nor are you naive. But that doesn't mean that there aren't people out there that are very good at fooling others, especially others that only look for the good in people."

"Thank you, but maybe you should wait until you hear the whole story before you decide," Jo said. She took a swallow of her drink and then sat it down. "Like I said, I met Jeffrey at a party. The next day there were flowers delivered to the critical care unit where I worked. I called to thank him, and the next thing I knew we were dating. I was wined and dined like a princess, and it was all like one big fairy tale. Just like our wedding. It was perfect. Everything was perfect, at least at first. That's how Jeffrey likes things to look. Perfect."

Casey straightened with this news. Jo had never mentioned being married. It seemed like there was a lot that she had never shared with him. Maybe she didn't trust him as much as he had thought.

"Tell me about these red flags," he said, trying to keep the hurt from his voice. This wasn't about him and his insecurities.

"Savannah's not really a large town, but it has its Who's Who crowd. My father and mother were always on the fringe of the upper society, which made my mother happy while leaving my father frustrated. Suddenly, I was surrounded by all these people who were beautiful and rich. Jeffrey wanted me to fit in. He said it was so I would be more comfortable around his friends. He made appointments for me at the best salons and the most elite boutiques. I tried to explain to him that I was a working woman who didn't have the time or money to keep up with his friend's wives, but it was as if I wasn't speaking. He just didn't get it. Finally, I had to put a stop to it. My credit card balances were rising faster than I could keep up. I tried to explain to him again, but he got mad and said I didn't appreciate everything he was doing for me. I didn't appreciate the fact that I was dating one of Savannah's most eligible bachelors." She stopped and took a sip of her drink.

From the little bit she had said, the man sounded like a real jerk. Couldn't he see that Jo didn't need any fancy salons or boutiques to make her beautiful? She was just as beautiful on the inside as she was on the outside, something that he found very rare in the women that he dated.

"I walked away then, but I couldn't help but think he might be right. I was twenty-four, and I had never had a serious relationship. Maybe I didn't know how. My parents loved him, and he was so charming most of the time. My mother had always told me that you have to pick your battles in a relationship, so when the flowers and the phone calls started again, I decided to give him another chance. I didn't really think he was a bad man, just a little full of himself. How things looked on the outside was very important to him. I thought I could change him. That I could show him that what was really important was what was on the inside. So I just ignored all the bad things and concentrated on the good I saw in him. The next thing I knew, we were married and living in an upscale subdivision. It was good at first."

"We'd only been married six months when he decided I would quit my job. But this time I pushed back. I loved my job as a nurse. I didn't want to quit. I had a career plan with the goal to become a flight nurse, so I chose to ignore him every time he brought it up. That's when he got physical. He didn't like me not doing what I was told to do."

Casey had known this was coming. He'd seen the fear in her eyes grow as she had told the story, as if she was living through it again. She didn't have to say anything more for him to understand that she hadn't shared the worst of her story.

"So, you left him," Casey said. "Good for you. It takes a lot of courage to walk out of an abusive relationship."

"Don't try to make me a hero, I wasn't," Jo said.

Casey thought about disagreeing with her, but decided now wasn't the time. Right now, he needed to know if what he feared, that she was in danger from the jerk who'd hurt her, was the reason for her sudden need to leave.

"So, this man, Jeffrey—" just the name left a bad taste in his mouth "—I take it he's giving you trouble."

"Oh, yes," Jo said, sarcasm dripping on each word, "from the phone call I received yesterday, I know he's definitely determined to give me trouble. When I pressed charges, he lost his job. When he was sentenced to five years for domestic battery, he lost his license."

"When does he get out?" he asked. They would need to be ready.

"Apparently, he was released a few months early for good behavior. He said the first thing he saw was a picture of me at Alex and Summer's wedding in Soura. Seeing me happy in my new life didn't sit well with him. Why should I be happy when his life has fallen apart? Now he's planning a trip to the Keys to 'see' me to talk about our marriage."

"You're still married?" This whole story was a lot to take in, but thinking of Jo still married to this jerk? That was too much.

"Of course not," she said. "But he fought against the divorce. Fortunately, I had a good lawyer, my dad, and the judge in the case granted me the divorce immediately."

"Did he threaten to hurt you?" Casey asked. He knew she had skimmed over the abuse. Jo was a strong woman. He'd seen her handle some of their most difficult patients while never losing her cool. She wouldn't want to remember the times when she had been the victim, and he would never ask her to relive them.

"No. He seems to think that he can talk me into going back to Savannah with him. It won't be until I tell him no that he'll begin with the threats. And if that doesn't work..." She didn't finish the sentence. She didn't have to. They both knew what she had been unable to say.

She stood and walked a few feet past him before turning around. "And now you know why I can't stay. Maybe I'm a coward, but I can't go through that again. I can't take the chance that he'll..." Her voice trailed off again.

She was afraid of the man because he had hurt her, both physically and emotionally, and she had good reasons to be. Who was he or anyone else to judge her as a coward? She'd survived the abusive relationship and found her way to Key West. To a new life where she had felt safe.

And he wasn't going to let her leave the life she had made for herself because some bully of a man had it in his mind that he could come here and take her back. "I won't let him hurt you. You know that."

"I knew you'd say that. That's why I didn't want to tell you. I don't want to get you involved in this," Jo said, before turning her back to him. He watched as her arms came around her body as if to hold herself together.

Unable to stop himself, he went to her and put his arms around her, pulling her back against him. "I'm already involved. We're a team. You know that. Alex and Summer, they'll feel the same way once we tell them what's going on. Katie and Dylan, Roy, none of us are going to sit around and let this guy bully you."

She pulled away from him, and he had to let her go even though he wanted to keep her close to him where he knew she would be safe.

"Exactly. And if Alex and Summer get involved, the next thing you know they'll be in the press and Jeffrey will be turning everything around until he's the victim. That's what he did in the divorce. He was the poor heartbroken husband and I was the gold digger, even though I asked for nothing from our divorce. He'll drag them into this mess, and that's the last thing the two of them need when they're trying to stay out of the limelight and raise their babies." The more she talked, the angrier she was getting. The old Jo was back, and he couldn't be happier to see her. "And you. I won't have you getting hurt because of me either."

He came to stand next to her and looked down. "I can take care of myself. Besides, I doubt this Jeffrey would be willing to go up against me. He's a bully who wants to prey on someone smaller than himself. Once he sees me he'll back off. That's why you're moving in with me."

"What?" Jo asked, looking up at him.

"It's the easiest solution. You move in with me and when your ex-husband shows up, he'll have no choice but to run back home."

"It's also only a temporary solution. He might leave when he sees you, but he'll come back. As long as he knows he can get to me, he'll return. I can't live looking over my shoulder for him. I need to leave before he gets here. I need to go somewhere he won't look for me. Maybe Mexico."

"Mexico? Really?"

"His legal buddies couldn't help him there, and I don't think he'll take a chance of ending up in one of their prisons."

Casey shook his head at her. "Are you listening to yourself? The Jo I know would never let a man like this guy run her out of town."

"The Jo you know wouldn't have married him either. But I did. I'm the woman who married a man who had all the signs of being controlling and abusive, and now I have to live with it."

"For how long, Jo? And at what cost? You're the victim. You don't deserve to be punished. But he does. Stay here. Let me help you. We don't have to bring anyone else into it. Stay and fight. I've got your back. Together we make a good team."

Jo looked at the man who meant more to her than just about anyone. Only her brother and sister had fought for her, at least at first. Once their eyes had been opened to the danger their daughter was in, her parents stood by her. Part of her still resented the fact that it had taken an injury bad enough to send her to the emergency room to make them see how bad things were. Not that she could blame them. They too had been fooled by Jeffrey's charm and polite manners.

But Casey believed her and wanted to help her. It made her want to be the woman he believed her to be. A woman who would stay and fight for herself. She hadn't been that woman when she'd left Savannah. Then she'd been afraid to even trust her own judgment. She'd made a mistake, a big one. What was there to keep her from making another one? What if she was making a mistake running away now? How could she know the right thing to do?

"If I stay, what can I do to make Jeffrey not come back?" she asked as she walked over to the small table and sat. The sleepless hours the night before were catching up with her. She felt as if she had just finished a marathon only to find that she still had another mile to run before she could rest.

"First you pack a bag, and then we get out

of here," Casey said, picking up the glasses off the table and heading inside.

"He just called last night. I don't think he'll be here this soon." Though hadn't she thought it was him at the door when Casey had shown up?

"If I go along with this, how are we going to explain to everyone that I've moved in with you without telling them about Jeffrey? They're bound to be curious. And what about Alex? He's going to have questions about why I've suddenly decided to stay," Jo said as she followed him inside.

And Summer? If her friend found out that it was a picture of Jo in her husband's family palace that had gotten Jeffrey's attention, she'd think it was all her fault. Summer and Alex were already concerned about how their private lives could spill over into their work lives and that of their coworkers.

"I've got an idea. How about we discuss it when we get to my place?" Casey asked.

"Okay," she said as she headed into her bedroom. She'd already packed most of her clothes into a large suitcase. She'd left only her flight clothes hanging in her closet, unable to throw them away. Unable to let go of what they stood for, the life she'd made and the job she loved. Grabbing those, she pushed her rolling case toward Casey, who picked it up with one hand while grabbing a mesh tote that held most of her shoes. She wouldn't need all of this for the short amount of time she was at Casey's, but she was too tired to go through it. She could just live out of her suitcase for a while. Besides, Casey's extra bedroom was only a small loft with an even smaller closet. But she'd make it work. She had to if she wanted to stay and face her ex-husband.

Because Casey was right, this was her best chance to make Jeffrey leave her alone once and for all. No, there were no guarantees, but at least with Casey's help she had a chance at finally feeling safe.

Safety. After her marriage, she had never taken it for granted again. It meant everything when you found yourself huddled in a corner afraid for your life.

While she packed up the things Moose would need, including the stuffed duck that he slept with every night, Casey helped her get everything into her car.

As she drove out of the parking lot, she

looked back at her apartment. It wasn't the nicest place on the island. It wasn't even in the best part of the island. There were no scenic views or beach access, but it had been hers. Of course, she'd be back. Moving in with Casey was just a temporary answer to her problems. Once she had handled the situation with Jeffrey, she'd move back and be just as happy as she had been before.

Living with Casey might be the right answer for now, but she knew there would be drawbacks. Because no matter how much she told herself that Casey was only letting her stay to help out a friend, part of her, the dangerous part, the part that replayed every dream in which he had played the leading role, was looking forward to living with Casey a little too much.

# CHAPTER THREE

ONCE SHE GAVE in to Casey and agreed to take
his bedroom while he took the loft, the fact
that Moose would have trouble fitting up the
stairs being the deciding factor, they brought
in her bags and she unpacked what she would
need for the next day. It wasn't until she found
Casey asleep on the couch that she remembered that he had worked the night shift before he'd come over to check on her.

She should have felt uncomfortable watching him sleep. Hadn't she woken up with Jeffrey standing over her, watching her sleep?
She shivered with the memory of feeling so
helpless.

But this was different. Innocent. Just a
friend admiring how sweet he looked with
his feet hanging off the end of the couch and
his arms wrapped around a pillow. His face
was relaxed. His guard was down. Both were

something that she saw very seldom. He slept like a babe without a care in the world. His blond curls, which always looked as if they needed cutting, had fallen over his eyes, and his mouth was curved with a secret smile.

He was such a beautiful man, though most people were more impressed with his size. More than once they'd been stopped by a tourist who had confused him with a national football player. They were always surprised when he told them that he was actually a local nurse. People just couldn't see such a big man taking care of their sick loved ones. They were so wrong. This man had a heart for caring for others as big as his six-foot-five frame and a commitment to do what was right as wide as his shoulders. What he was doing for her was just an example of how caring he could be.

And what was she doing? Oh, just standing there admiring the view while he slept. Nope, not creepy at all. When Moose moved to lie down beside him, Jo went into the kitchen and began to make a meal, something a lot more productive than staring at Casey. By the time she heard him shuffle into the room, she had a nice pico de gallo salsa made as well as all the toppings for fish tacos ready.

"I just have to panfry the fish," she said, turning to see him leaning against the counter while his heavy-lidded eyes studied her.

"Something wrong?" she asked, then realized what she had done. "I'm sorry. I didn't mean to take over your kitchen. I should have asked first."

"Why would you ask? We've cooked in this kitchen together before. And you don't need to ask. Haven't you always made yourself at home here? Why would that change now?"

She knew he was right, but somehow this felt different. Changing from welcomed friend to roommate was going to take a little getting used to. At least for her.

"Well, if it's not me taking over your kitchen, what is it? Something has you thinking very hard. Is it regrets? You know I'd understand if you've changed your mind about all of this."

"I haven't changed my mind. Nor will I. You're stuck with me by your side until this is over. I'm just wondering if you are going to change your mind once I tell you what I think we should do." Crossing his arms, his eyes never left her. It seemed that whatever it was he planned, his mind was set.

She slid the red fish into the oven before turning back to him. "So tell me."

"You remember that girlie movie you made me watch a couple months ago?" he asked. "The one with the woman who's invited to her ex-boyfriend's wedding so she hires a co-worker to pretend to be her fiancé?"

"First, I didn't make you watch it. It was my turn to pick the movie. You could have left if you didn't want to see it. Besides, I'd watched that ancient horror flick with you the week before. Second, that was a movie. No one does that in real life." She started to laugh then stopped. One look at his stubborn jaw told her he wasn't kidding. "You don't seriously think anyone would believe we were…are…"

She couldn't even say it let alone do it. Pretending to be more than friends with Casey would be very dangerous, and she already had enough danger in her life.

"It makes perfect sense. You can tell Alex that we had a fight, something like, 'Things between me and Casey changed, and I didn't know how to handle it.'" He spoke in a high-pitched voice as he tried to imitate her. She wasn't sure if he thought he was being funny, but she wasn't amused. Not by any of this.

"So I call Alex and tell him that I've come to my senses and see now that I belong with you. Oh, and also, we're engaged to be married?"

"Yes, exactly," Casey said. His face lit up with the smile of a man who had just won a great battle. How could such a smart man come up with such a plan?

"You don't really think he's going to believe me, do you?" Though her own heart beat a little faster at the thought of being engaged to Casey. Apparently, they both had a problem with separating reality from fantasy.

"What other explanation for your change of plans and moving in with me will they have? Unless you want to tell them the truth."

No. Telling her friends and coworkers would just put more people at risk. "I can't do that. Not now. Maybe later. Maybe if I manage to get Jeffrey out of my life for good, I'll tell them. But right now, especially for Alex and Summer, they are better off staying out of this."

"So, you agree?" he asked.

"I think getting people to believe that we are suddenly engaged would be a stretch. You've been too adamant about remaining the most eligible bachelor of the crew for too long. You have a different woman every season. It's who you are."

"I'm not that bad," he said, then grimaced. "Well, I haven't been lately."

A look came over Casey's face that she couldn't identify. He'd always taken pride in his bachelor status, something that she had teased him about for years. Why now did he look like he had lost his best friend? Was it because of her?

"I can't do it," she said. "It's not fair to you. I'll go back to the apartment. I'll be okay. If Jeffrey shows up, I'll call the police."

"We've already been through this. The best thing is to show Jeffrey that you are not alone. Let him see that you can take care of yourself, but also let him see that I have your back. What better way to show the man you're not scared of him than to show him you've moved on? You don't want Jeffrey to think that you've been waiting for him to show up and take you away. Show the jerk that you've moved on in every way. That you're involved with someone else now."

"He'll hate that," she admitted. And once he got a look at Casey he'd think twice about coming after her. "I can agree to everything except the fake engagement. I don't think it's necessary. We can pretend to have suddenly taken a romantic interest in each other and even stretch it a bit that we're trying out living together, but that's the most that I think anyone will believe. Also, that way when Jeffrey is taken care of, we can go back to our old relationship without any explanation. People will just think things didn't work out romantically, but that we are still friends. Agreed?"

Casey hesitated for a moment before offering her his hand. "Agreed."

Placing her hand in his, she felt that irritating hum of her body whenever she and Casey touched. She agreed with him that a united front would be the best defense from her ex-husband. She just hoped it was worth risking her friendship with Casey.

Because no matter what happened between her and Jeffrey, she knew that her relationship with her best friend might never be the same. How could it be? He knew all her secrets now. Would he ever again see her as the strong woman she'd worked so hard to become? Or would he always see her as the victim she used to be? Even though doubt and shame still filled her when she thought of the way she'd let Jeffrey manipulate her, deep inside she knew she wasn't that person anymore. She'd changed. Now she just had to find some way to prove it to Casey. And she would, no matter what it took.

Jo walked out of Alex's office feeling like a terrible employee and an even worse friend. In a perfect world, you didn't have to hide parts of your life from the people you cared about. But her life hadn't been perfect in a long time. And right now, she couldn't let the guilt she felt talk her into turning around and walking back into the office and spilling the truth. She and Casey had a plan, and she would stick to it.

Her radio went off, drawing her mind back to where it needed to be. She wouldn't let the drama in her life overflow into her job. That would be dangerous for both her patients and her career.

As she listened to the report of a Jet Ski accident near Fort Zachary, she caught up with Casey and their pilot, James, as they were headed out the door. Once in the helicopter, Jo buckled herself into her harness and put on her helmet.

During liftoff, she listened as James got more information on the location of the accident. From the report, it sounded like it would be a "scoop and run" call due to the traumatic head injury the patient might have suffered—as long as they could get the patient stabilized. Time meant everything when you were dealing with a head injury, and without a neurosurgeon available on the island, they'd be flying straight to the nearest Miami hospital that would be able to accept them.

"Everything okay?" Casey asked.

"It's all good," Jo said. Looking over at him, she gave him a thumbs-up. She had known Casey was watching her and had to be anxious to know how things had gone with Alex. It wasn't that either of them thought Alex wouldn't let her rescind her resignation, but they also knew that he would want more of a reason than she was able to give.

Fortunately, Alex had taken her excuse of just needing to make some changes in her life without much questioning. His eyes had told her that he knew there was more to the story than she was saying, but he was too polite to ask. Not that he would be wondering for long. It would get out that she was "involved" with Casey eventually, and rumors would be flying about the change in their relationship. It was exactly what they wanted. By the time Jeffrey showed up, they needed everyone to believe that she and Casey were a couple so that they could fool him.

She hoped to have some warning before her ex showed up, but so far Jeffrey hadn't tried to contact her again. She couldn't help but think he was dragging the suspense out, thinking that she would be cowering somewhere, afraid to go out. It was the kind of mental game he liked to play with her.

But he was in for a surprise this time. A big one.

She looked over to where Casey was setting up an IV bag for infusion, and her lips curled up in an unexpected grin. She was almost looking forward to the look in Jeffrey's eyes when he saw all six feet five inches of her muscled friend standing beside her.

The dispatcher informed them of the receiving hospital that they would be transporting to, and Jo returned her attention to preparing the items they would need for their patient. They began their descent to a location that Fire and Rescue had cleared, and Jo could see a small crowd gathered around the EMTs.

Her body went on alert as soon as the skids touched the ground. Taking the lead, she grabbed their supply bag while Casey followed behind with the stretcher.

"Jo. Casey. Nice of you to join us," one of the EMTs said as the crowd moved back, giving her the first view of their patient. No more than twenty, the young woman was conscious though there was a lot of blood in the sand surrounding her head.

"Nice to see you, too. Who's our patient?"

"This is Zoe," the EMT said, and Jo listened as he began to give a full report on the accident and the patient's injuries. From the description of the collision, the woman was lucky that she hadn't been killed when she had crossed into the path of the other Jet Ski.

"The other person?" Jo asked as she knelt beside the young woman's head.

"The patient's boyfriend, Daniel. He's

shaken up—" the EMT looked over at the young man crouched near the woman "—but no injuries that we can see."

"Hi, Zoe, my name is Jo and this is Casey. Have you ever been in a helicopter before?"

"Yes," said the woman. The word came out slow, which was cause for concern that this was more than just a head laceration. There was a good chance it was a sign of a serious head injury. But when Jo checked Zoe's pupils, they were reactive.

"Can you tell me your name and where you are?" Jo asked as Casey began to apply the electro pads so that they could monitor their patient's vital signs.

The woman looked over to the young man beside her. He was as pale as the white sand under their feet, and his eyes were wide with shock. "Her name is Zoe. We're just here in Key West for the week. We're getting married next year when I get out of college, and we wanted to check out the wedding venues. Can you tell me if she's going to be okay? Do I need to call her parents?"

"Well, that's what we are here for. To make sure she's okay. And, yes, I would call her parents. But what we need now is for her to answer our questions. It will help us and the doctor know how serious her injury is."

"Sorry," the young man said, before looking back at Zoe.

"No problem," Casey said from beside him. "We understand you're trying to help."

"Zoe, can you tell me where you are right now and what month it is?" Jo asked again.

"Key West, and it's August," the woman answered.

"That's good. Real good. Now, can you tell me if you hurt anywhere?" Jo asked, pulling back a dressing that had been applied to Zoe's head. There was a laceration across her forehead that was still oozing blood. She didn't see any deformity of the skull, but without a CT scan there wasn't any way of knowing what other damage could be present.

"My head hurts. Bad. Like the worst headache ever. And my stomach feels sick," Zoe answered.

"Vital signs are stable," Casey told Jo as he watched the monitor screen. "Normal sinus rhythm in the nineties."

A little fast but it that was to be expected.

"O2 saturation?" she asked.

"Good. Ninety-eight percent."

"We'll give you something for the nausea as soon as we get you loaded in the helicopter," Casey told her.

"Can you give her something for the pain?" Daniel asked. Some color had returned to his face, but he was still in shock. He was so young. The both of them were. Too young to be graduating from college let alone getting married. Not that she had been much older when she'd married Jeffrey.

But she couldn't judge every marriage by her own. She knew that, though sometimes she found it difficult. It was just instinctual to want to protect others from her mistake.

"Nothing for pain yet," Casey answered for her. "We have to be able to do the neuro assessments that are necessary right now. Even a slight change can make a difference."

While Jo and one of the EMTs placed a C-collar to stabilize Zoe's neck, Casey gave the fiancé the information on the hospital where they would be taking her. But when Daniel began to follow them to the helicopter, Jo called one of the EMTs to the side.

"Can you check over this young man before he leaves? I don't like the idea of him driving without being sure he's okay," she said.

When the EMT nodded and headed toward Daniel, she and Casey rushed their patient into the helicopter and prepared for flight. In minutes they were airborne and headed to a Miami trauma center where she hoped the neurosurgeon would have good news for the young couple. By the time they landed, Jo was feeling even more hopeful. Zoe's vital signs had remained stable and her neuro assessments were unchanged. Maybe she'd be one of the lucky ones.

They rolled into the trauma room with the trauma doctor waiting for them, and while Casey began to report off to the hospital team, Jo finished their charting and went to drop it off with the unit coordinator. When she returned, she found the trauma room empty except for Casey and one of the emergency room nurses—Sarah? Or was her name Susan?

"They've taken Zoe to CT," Casey said, before clearing his throat. Why did his voice sound so strained? Then she noticed he was staring at the doorway, as if he was about to make a run for it at any moment.

"Did something happen?" Jo asked, afraid

Zoe had deteriorated in the few minutes she'd been gone.

"No, she's fine," said the nurse, whose name tag read Sarah. Her gaze never left Casey. "I was just telling Casey that I'm going to be in Key West for a vacation in a few days."

It had taken a few minutes for Jo to recognize the woman, but now that she did the tense atmosphere in the empty trauma room made sense. Sarah and Casey had dated briefly a few months earlier, and she had not been happy when Casey had told her he had no plans for anything serious.

It had been just one of many such conversations that Casey had relayed to her over a drink at their favorite tiki bar. Jo had tried to support him and see his side. She knew that he never meant to hurt anyone he dated, and most of the women he chose to go out with were just looking to have fun like he was. It was the other women, the ones who thought they could end Casey's self-declared eternal bachelorhood that bothered him the most. He just couldn't understand why they thought he was looking for anything more.

Because of her history, Jo had understood

the dangers of someone becoming obsessed with you, and on more than one occasion she had advised him to cut all contact with the woman before things could get ugly.

"That's nice," Jo said. She ignored the little jealous devil that seemed to sit on one of her shoulders every time she had to talk to one of Casey's girlfriends. For the first time, she wondered if Casey had ever thought it strange that she had never been overly friendly with any of them. "I sent the paperwork and radioed James that we were headed up to the roof."

"Great, we better get going then," Casey said, all but running out of the room, not bothering to tell the other woman goodbye.

"Hold on," Jo said as she caught up with him at the elevator. "What was that about?"

"Nothing. It was nothing," Casey said, though Jo noticed that he was watching the hallway as if he thought someone might be following behind her.

"I didn't mean to interrupt," she said, not sure if Casey was upset at her or at Sarah.

"There was nothing for you to interrupt," Casey said, his tone defensive.

"Okay. I get it. It's none of my business,"

Jo said as she got into the elevator that would take them to the roof, leaving Casey to follow her. Was he upset because he wasn't free to see Sarah now?

"I'm sorry. Sarah cornered me in the room and started telling me how much she's missed me. She wanted to see me when she comes down to the Keys on some girls' weekend trip she has planned. I didn't know what to say. I mean we were at work. I couldn't be rude."

"What did you want to say?" Jo asked, trying to keep all emotion out of her voice. It wasn't fair to Casey that he'd become saddled with Jo's problems if it came between him and Sarah making up, though Jo found it hard to believe that was in Casey's plans at all. Once he ended a relationship, he moved on. He never seemed to look back at anything in his life. He lived his life with no regrets while she lived with her regrets on a daily basis.

"You know I'm not any good dealing with women when they get all emotional. I don't know what to say."

But he sure knew how to run away whenever a woman declared she wanted more than a good time from him.

"If you didn't want to see her again, you

could have just told her you were involved with someone else." It shouldn't bother her that he hadn't spoken up and told Sarah about her and Casey's new "relationship." It wasn't like they were a real couple. Instead of being resentful that he hadn't been willing to claim that he was involved with her, she should feel bad that she was putting him in this position.

"I was just trying to get out of there before things became any more uncomfortable," he said, walking out onto the roof as soon as the elevator doors opened, leaving her behind to regret that she'd even mentioned their pretend relationship.

Casey was quiet on the trip back to headquarters, which started to worry Jo. Was he mad at her because of what she'd said? She had caught a glimpse of the look Sarah had given him as he walked away. It was plain to see that she was not giving up on Casey.

She should feel bad, if not for Sarah at least for Casey. But seeing the way the woman had looked at him had made Jo want to yell "stay away, he's mine" at the top of her lungs.

Guilt began to eat at her. She didn't have any right to feel possessive of Casey. She needed to remember that this pretense would be over soon. What if she was reading the whole situation wrong? Maybe Casey had been happy to find out Sarah was going to be on the island and then had remembered that with the complication Jo had brought into his life he wasn't free to spend his time with her.

But what could she do about it? It was too late to change their minds now. She'd reassured Alex that she would not be leaving the island. She couldn't turn back. He wouldn't agree to it if she asked him to. They'd started on a path that would hopefully set her free from her ex-husband, and until that was done they'd both be living a necessary lie.

She just had to keep reminding herself that this was all make-believe. She'd let Casey ride in like a knight in shining armor to rescue her because he was her friend. She had to protect that friendship, even if it meant she had to protect it from herself.

# CHAPTER FOUR

THERE WAS SOMEONE knocking on the door. Only the sound didn't seem to be coming from the right location.

Jo opened her eyes at the same time that Moose chose to send out an alarming bark that would have woken her whole apartment building. But she wasn't at her apartment, which explained why the sound was coming from somewhere unfamiliar.

"Wait a moment," Jo told Moose as he began scratching at the bedroom door. Except for her hair, which felt like a nest on top of her head, she was decent enough in an oversize T-shirt and bike shorts.

Opening the bedroom door, she headed to the front door, only to stop when she recognized the voice on the other side.

"Open up, Casey," Summer called from the other side. "We need to talk."

Jo turned toward the staircase leading up to the loft and wasn't surprised to see Casey standing at the top of the stairs. He was shirtless, with a pair of pajama pants riding low on his hips. Jo wanted to forget her friend at the door and just spend an hour, or maybe two, enjoying the view.

She blinked and tried to clear her head. Sharing a place with Casey should have come with a warning label.

She made her eyes move up to Casey's face, and was relieved to see that he hadn't noticed her moment of weakness. "It's Summer. What do we do?"

Casey's eyes brightened a moment before he turned before disappearing back into the loft. "Answer the door, Jo. I'm pretty sure it's you she's looking for."

"Jo, is that you?" Summer called from the other side of the door. The woman had to have supersonic hearing.

"Casey, where are you going?" Jo called up the stairs. "What am I supposed to tell her?"

He didn't answer her, making it clear that he was leaving her on her own to handle their friend. With everything he had done for her, she couldn't be mad. She was closer to Summer than Casey, so it would seem right for her to handle all the questions she was bound to have about finding Jo there. Of course, Jo could pretend that she had just stopped over to visit. But that would just be putting off the inevitable.

With that thought, Jo opened the door. Summer stood on the other side, alone.

"Where are the babies?" Jo asked.

"Alex's mom is in town. She was thrilled for a chance to watch them," Summer said as she looked inside the door. "Where's Casey?"

"He's asleep. In case you don't know, we worked last night."

"I know that," Summer said as Jo stepped back to let her in. "Hey, Moose."

"Then why are you here? I can't believe you asked your mother-in-law to keep the babies so you could visit with Casey," Jo said as Summer gave Moose a head rub.

"Maybe the better question is, what are you doing here?" Summer asked, her face coming alive with a mischievous grin. "Are the two of you having a sleepover?"

Jo started to deny Summer's suggestion then thought of Casey up in the loft listening to them. He wanted her to take the lead on this, so she would. And if she had a bit of fun with it, it was his own fault.

"Shh, don't wake him up," Jo said, looking to where she had shut the bedroom door. "We were both exhausted when we finally went to sleep."

Jo watched as Summer took in the innuendo she had planted. Summer's naughty smile let her know right when her friend had fallen for it.

"I knew it. When your neighbor said he saw a blond giant helping you load a suitcase in your car, I knew it had to be Casey. What happened? Did you finally tell him how you feel?" Summer said as she took a seat on the couch. Jo's stomach dropped to her feet. Had Casey heard that?

"What are you talking about?" Jo said as she kicked Summer's shin with her bare foot then took a seat beside her, grabbing her toes. "Ouch."

"What is wrong…oh…" Summer said, finally understanding. "So, what happened? I mean you must have decided that you feel something for him. You are *sleeping* here, right?"

"It's complicated," Jo said. Now that Summer had covered her slip, Jo was left not knowing how to proceed.

"It has to be if you were about to leave the island. I couldn't believe it when Alex told me. You leave Key West? It didn't make sense. I thought you were happy here." Summer said as she moved over and made room for Moose beside her.

"I am happy. I don't really know what I was thinking. It just seemed the only thing I could do at the time." At least that was the truth, even if it did lead Summer in a different direction. "But everything is settled. I understand what I need now."

"To make you happy?" Summer asked.

"Yes, to make me happy," Jo said. Getting rid of her fear of her ex-husband would make her very happy.

"I'm glad. For you and Casey. He's not been himself lately," Summer said, and then smiled. "And now I know why."

"You do?" Was there something going on with Casey that she didn't know about? Had his mood been a little more serious lately? A little less carefree?

"Sure. You don't think this thing between you two just happened, do you?"

If Summer only knew. Someday she'd tell her the truth. When everything was done and Jeffrey was out of her life for good, Jo would take Summer out to lunch and explain everything. Her friend wouldn't be happy, but of all the people she knew, Summer would understand. Her whole life had been opened up to the public when she became pregnant with Alex's babies. Now, as the princess of Soura, she fought to keep her life as private as possible.

"I've got to get back to the babies, and I know you need some more sleep," Summer said as she moved Moose's big head from her lap and stood. "Oh, and your neighbor wanted me to tell you he has a package that was left for you. He didn't want to leave it out when you didn't come home the other night."

Jo didn't mention the fact that she moved in with Casey. Now that Summer believed that they were an item, she didn't seem surprised that Jo was staying with Casey. And though she hated to think about what would happen when Jeffrey did show up, she wished he would just get it over with. Waiting for him while having to constantly lie to her friends wasn't the way she wanted to live her life.

Even worse was asking Casey to continue this farce with her. But what else could she do? If she was ever going to get Jeffrey to understand that she had moved on and would never let him into her life again, they needed to look like the happy couple. Jeffrey needed to believe that Casey was in her life for good and would be there to protect her if he tried to hurt or threaten her again.

If she knew her ex-husband, he was busy making plans on how he would intimidate her into doing whatever he wanted from her. The plan she and Casey had was her only defense, and she had no choice. They'd play the loving couple for everyone, and she'd do it with a smile on her face. She wouldn't give Jeffrey one reason to doubt them. Her ability to remain here with her friends demanded it.

"Sarah, again?" Jo asked, her voice sharp with aggravation.

In the three days since he'd seen Sarah at the hospital in Miami, she'd called him four times, each with a different excuse. And while he couldn't understand why Sarah insisted on calling when he'd made it plain to her that there was nothing left between them,

Jo's reaction seemed off. Was there something between the two women that he wasn't aware of? Or was this just another sign that he didn't understand women. He'd known enough of them that you'd think he'd have them all figured out by now. When he'd been younger, he'd been sure that he understood everything about them. Then Anna had run off and he'd been stunned. He'd never even known she was unhappy, though he would have sworn he knew everything about her. That was when he realized he knew absolutely nothing about women. And now, over ten years later, he still couldn't wrap his mind around what a confusing bunch they were.

But he'd always thought Jo was different. She'd always been so levelheaded. She didn't lose her temper and yell at him when he climbed into her car covered in sand from a volleyball match. She didn't pout when he was late for lunch because he stopped to help Ms. Terrie next door with her garden. She was different from all the women he dated. Except right now she wasn't acting very Jo-like at all.

"Sarah just wanted to update me on Zoe's condition. She got permission from her first," Casey said. And why he was defending Sarah? Maybe it was because he still felt bad about the way she'd taken it when he'd had to end things between them. Their relationship had no future. He still didn't understand how Sarah could have read anything more into it. But then, he didn't understand women.

"If that was all she wanted to do, she could have texted you," Jo said, before taking a sip of the wine he'd opened to go with the lasagna he had baked for their supper. "She's trying to start things back up again."

"Maybe," Casey said. Sarah had been very insistent that he know the hotel she would be staying at while in Key West. "But it's not going to happen. I was very open about the fact that I don't plan on getting seriously involved with anyone. Besides, now that—"

"Now that you're stuck with me as your pretend girlfriend?" Jo asked with sarcasm in her voice, which he had never heard before.

He stopped eating and studied her. Her face had been scrubbed to a healthy glow, and her hair, damp from a shower, had been pulled into a bun on the top of her head. She still looked tired, her eyes puffy from lack of sleep, but with them both coming off their second shift in three days it was to be expected. It was the stubborn look on her face that was a surprise. She had moved in with him three days ago, and she wasn't any happier about their arrangement now than she had been when he'd first suggested it. Was it because of this thing with Sarah? Or maybe it wasn't Sarah at all.

"Is that embarrassing for you?" he asked. Maybe dating him—pretend dating him—wasn't up to her normal standards. She'd married a lawyer. He was a small island nurse with no future of anything more.

"Are you kidding?" Her tired eyes sparkled with humor, and he relaxed. There was the Jo he knew and loved. "I'm the first woman you've let inside this place. I'll be envied by half the single women in the Keys."

"Just half?" he asked, getting the laugh he had intended from her.

"Okay, maybe two-thirds. There's probably already a betting pool going at work on how long this will last," Jo said. When the light went out of her eyes, he knew that she was once again thinking about Jeffrey and when he would appear.

"Is there a bet on who calls it off? You or

me?" Casey said, hoping to lighten things up again. When all he got from Jo was a quirk of her lips, he knew he had failed. "Quit worrying about it. Even if Jeffrey shows up, he'll go to your apartment first."

He could see that his words were not helping. "Let's stick the dishes in the dishwasher and go out."

"Now? Aren't you tired?" Jo asked.

"I got a good nap, and I think both of us would sleep better tonight if we got some fresh air. Don't you?"

In minutes they finished their meals and had the dishes taken care of and Moose loaded into Casey's truck. Not sure if Jo would be up to their usual crowd and the questions they were sure to ask now that it was out that the two of them were "dating," he headed to Key West Dog Beach.

While Moose had gotten his two walks a day while they were working, the big guy loved to run on the beach and he headed straight for the water the moment Jo let him out of the truck.

"We could be here for hours," Jo said as she watched Moose run through the waves.

"The only thing I have to do tomorrow is

work a dog food donation drive at the shelter," Casey said as he pulled a blanket from the oversize toolbox in his truck.

He took her hand as they waded through the deep sand. It was something he had done a hundred times, helping a woman this way, but it somehow felt different tonight. He knew that Jo was vulnerable. He'd noticed that she had mostly just moved her food around on her plate. Waiting for Jeffrey to make a move was getting to her, and Casey didn't like it.

"I don't understand why you're always working to help the shelter, but you refuse to get a dog of your own," Jo said.

"I got you Moose," he said. It was a long argument between the two of them. Jo didn't understand that the responsibility of a dog was something he wasn't prepared for. Having someone—or a dog—depend on you tied you down, and that wasn't for him.

"And I will always be grateful," Jo said, then groaned when the big dog rushed them, almost knocking her to the ground.

Casey easily caught her, pressing her to him as Moose ran circles around them, pouncing against them and almost taking them both down.

"Maybe he needs to go back to obedience classes," Jo said, then threw her arms around Casey as the dog made a jump into the air before running back to the surf.

Casey rested his chin against the top of her head and breathed in the floral scent of her hair along with the salty ocean water that Moose had splattered them with. "He's just enjoying himself. He's been cooped up in the house for the past couple of days. He'll calm down."

Jo pulled away, looking up at him with a smile that did something funny to his insides. What was this? It wasn't like this was the first time he'd given Jo a hug. But this? Again, this felt different. Scary. And totally inappropriate.

He stepped away from her and began searching for a flat piece of beach. With the help of the moon and stars shining over them, he found the perfect spot and spread out the blanket. If he sat a little closer to the edge, Jo didn't seem to notice.

"I can't believe I was going to leave this place," Jo said as she stretched out beside him and stared up at the moon. "I'm glad you talked me into staying. Into fighting to keep the life I have here. You're a good man, Casey Johnson."

"I'm glad you came to your senses." Casey couldn't admit that it had been for his own selfish reasons that he had worked so hard to keep her on the island. When he'd heard Jo was leaving, it had been like a punch in his gut. He'd been left behind by his high school sweetheart. His grandmother had passed away. Even his own parents had left the island for one of those adult only communities that Miami was famous for. All of those things had hurt him, though he'd never tell his parents. They were happy where they were, and it was a lot easier for them to live out their retirement on the mainland than it would have been for them to stay in the Keys.

But Jo leaving? He didn't know what he would have done if she had left him behind. She was an important part of his life. His constant support and companion. It was something that his girlfriends had never liked. And he'd never shared with Jo that she was one of the reasons that a lot of his relationships ended. It seemed asking a woman to accept his best friend was a woman was too much. Pointing out to them that it was a sexist attitude hadn't helped either. Nope, he'd never understand them.

"I never dreamed I would be living here, in Florida, let alone the Keys. I did dream of being a flight nurse. But that was before I met Jeffrey. He always thought it was a stupid goal."

"And you were going to just give up your dream for him?" Casey had a hard time imagining the woman Jo had been back then. It was as if the woman she had been had risen from the ashes of her marriage and taken on another life. Life did change people. He'd seen that and experienced it himself. Once he'd been a young man wanting nothing more than to settle down and raise a family. He couldn't imagine being that person again.

"Did you always want to be a flight nurse? Is that why you got out of the coast guard?"

"I always wanted to live here on the island. I was lucky to get stationed here for the first two years, and then I was stationed in Ketchikan, Alaska, for the last three years. It's beautiful country. I saw sights that I never dreamed I'd see. But it wasn't home."

He leaned back and relaxed beside her. This felt right. This was easy. Talking to Jo had always been easy. He thought of the way she'd been when Sarah had called. He knew she was just being protective and now, knowing what she had went through with her ex-husband, he understood why she'd always warned him when a woman's interest began to cross the line into stalking. He was lucky to have her in his life.

"Promise me that you won't ever leave without talking to me first," he said, not sure why he needed to have the promise. She'd already agreed to stay and face Jeffrey.

"I told you I was sorry. I wouldn't have left without talking to you. It was wrong, and I was being a coward not telling you first," she said. "But I promise. If I feel I don't have any other choice but to leave, I'll talk to you first."

"Now, you have to promise me that we won't let all this drama with Jeffrey destroy our friendship. If you change your mind about faking this romance with me, you have to tell me." Jo turned her head to his and the moonlight washed over her face. Her dark eyes searched his, for what he wasn't sure. Why was she so afraid that something would come between the two of them?

"I promise, but I won't change my mind.

This will work, Jo. Once Jeffrey comes and sees that you've made this new life he'll have no choice but to leave. Having me standing beside you will show him that you're not alone. He'll leave as fast as he can get a plane out of here, I guarantee."

"I hope you're right. I wish he'd come tomorrow so we can get this over with. Lying to our friends, pretending to be something we're not, it's all wrong."

He covered her hand with his and squeezed it. He knew she was nervous. He couldn't imagine facing someone who had threatened and abused you.

When her fingers locked with his and she laid her head on his shoulder, his body hardened and his stomach shuddered. He froze, unable to move, while his brain tried to talk some sense into the rest of his body. It was an old fight between the two of them. His body insisting on its attraction to Jo while his brain accepted that their friendship meant there was no place for anything else. Years ago, when Jo had first arrived in Key West, before they'd built the friendship they had now, he'd asked her out. Her sharp "no," before she'd gone on to explain that she needed a friend more than anything else had been enough to stop any ideas he'd had about anything romantic happening between them.

And she'd been right. He found the relationship they had was much more rewarding than he'd ever had with one of his girlfriends. That took her off his list of available women. So why was he having this primal reaction to her now? Was his body getting confused by all this pretending they were doing?

He removed his hand from hers and sat up, casually putting some room between them. Maybe Jo was right. This pretending to be romantically and physically involved could be dangerous. The best thing for both of them was for Jeffrey to come so their lives could go back to normal before he did something that they both might regret.

# CHAPTER FIVE

"WHAT ARE THE two of you doing?" Alex asked from the kitchen that opened out into the multiuse room.

Jo stomped down on where Casey's instep had been just seconds before then turned and pushed the palm of her right hand at his nose, stopping only inches from making contact.

"I'm just teaching Jo a few self-defense moves," Casey said as he stepped back from Jo's outstretched hand.

She hadn't been sure what Casey had in mind when he started moving the furniture to the side of the room. Dancing? Aerobics? Yoga? With Casey, you never knew.

But no, the man was on a mission to keep her safe, and teaching her to protect herself was his goal. She didn't want to break it to him that she had taken a defense class before coming to the island. Then it had been her brother who had insisted she learn some moves to protect herself. It wasn't that she didn't know the moves. It was that she panicked where Jeffrey was concerned. The memories of what he'd done to her in the past seemed to surround her. They had kept her frozen in place with fear until it was too late to fight back.

But it wouldn't be that way this time. Not with Casey backing her up.

"Nice," Alex said. "Maybe I should get Summer a class on defense for her birthday."

"I don't think that would be a good idea." While she might enjoy the class, Jo was sure that Summer was expecting something a little more romantic.

"Jewelry. Women love jewelry," Casey said as he began to move the furniture back into place.

"She has lots of jewelry and she barely wears any of it," Alex said. "She says she never has anyplace to wear it to that wouldn't make her look ridiculous."

"So take her out somewhere she can wear it. There's a new French restaurant downtown that would be perfect." And Jo knew Summer would love it. Alex's wife had become a total foodie since spending time in his father's palace where the chefs had gone out of their way to spoil their princess.

"We both agreed after the last time we took the twins out that we wouldn't do it again until they were in college," Alex said.

Jo had heard about that experience and knew that Alex was only partly kidding. "We can keep the babies for you. Just schedule it during a time the two of us are both off."

"We?" Casey asked. "I don't do babies."

"*We* do babies every day," Jo said as the radio clipped to her flight pants went off.

Pulling her arms into the top of the suit she'd unzipped and left hanging around her waist when they'd come in from their last flight, she grabbed the bottle of water she'd left on the floor and rushed for the door while the dispatcher was still giving the location of the fire they were to respond to.

"I hate fires," Casey said as they buckled up and began to ready their equipment.

Jo understood. The smell of burned flesh made her stomach sick, and more than once she'd resorted to a mask lined with menthol salve. "Hopefully everyone got out."

But Jo's heart sank when she saw the tall,

bright orange flames towering into the sky above the building. It would have been full of people as it was still early in the afternoon as their helicopter flew over the island.

"The police have cordoned off a place at a strip mall just north of the fire's location," the dispatcher said.

"Visibility is good from up here, though the smoke seems to be spreading," Roy, their pilot, said. "ETA two minutes. I'll be waiting for them to let me know it's all clear."

"Have they radioed in what we'll be transporting?" Casey asked the dispatcher.

"From what I've been told, you will be emergency backup at this time. No victims or fatalities identified as of now," the dispatcher said.

"I say we take the stretcher just in case," Jo said as she stuffed extra dressings into the big duffel bag that held all their equipment.

"I'll take one of the oxygen tanks too. There could be some inhalation problems for the responders," Casey said.

The moment the skids hit the ground Jo unloaded with Casey right behind her.

"I'm to take you to the EMTs," a young police officer said as she joined them.

They followed closely behind her, weaving through the crowd of onlookers that had formed around the engulfed building. Jo recognized the place as Lucy's, a place where their whole crew often met. "This will break Lucy's and Darren's heart."

"Let's just pray they both got out," Casey said.

"That's where they want you," the officer said, pointing to where two crews of EMTs were treating people. "I'm going to get some help to get the crowd back so you'll have more room."

"Thank you," Casey said. "We appreciate the help."

They split up as Casey headed toward the EMT crews and Jo started toward the local fire chief, a man she had met, unfortunately, on too many flights.

"How many men do you still have in the building?" she asked, stepping over a long thick hose that ran from the fire truck where they stood toward the pub. There was no way they could save Lucy's place, so if anyone was inside the building it had to be in the hope of rescuing someone.

"Only two left inside. The wait staff claim

that one of the owners went toward the kitchen where the fire started instead of out the front. They've got two minutes left before I call them back."

So either Lucy or Darren was still in the building? Knowing the two of them, it would be Lucy. She loved their pub. She'd told Jo once that having the pub had been what had saved her when her first husband died. She'd bought the building with the insurance money she'd received after his death and moved to Key West to open a pub. It had been their dream for years, and she had been determined to live the life she knew he wanted for her. It was here she had met the second love of her life, Darren. Jo had loved to hear that story with its happily-ever-after ending. It had to be wonderful to be loved like that.

The smoke coming off the building was intensifying, and as the firemen worked to keep the flames down as best they could, she was forced to move back. There would be no happily-ever-after today.

Two large men exited the building carrying a body. When the person in their arms coughed, Jo took a much-needed breath, coughing as the smoke entered her own lungs, then followed the firemen to where the EMTs waited.

Casey and one of the EMTs made it to the firemen first, and Casey helped them lower the patient onto their flight stretcher. Though everything on the person was covered in black soot and a towel was wrapped around the face, Jo could see a mop of wet gray hair and knew it was Lucy.

As the other EMTs rushed to care for the firemen that had over heated, Jo and Casey started their assessment. Neither of them had any doubt that Lucy was in critical condition from the smoke she'd inhaled. That would make her their patient to get to Miami as soon as possible.

"Lucy," Jo said as she unwrapped the towel the rest of the way from her head, "it's Jo and Casey. Do you know where you are?"

"Jo?" the woman asked, then started coughing. "Heli-Care Jo?"

"Yes, ma'am. Casey is here too." Jo examined the woman, peeling back a partially burned apron carefully. Under the apron, there was a golf-ball-sized hole where a deep burn was visible on Lucy's chest.

"I'm going to put a mask over your face

now to give you some oxygen to help you breathe," Casey said, from beside her.

"Casey? My boy, Casey?" the woman asked.

As he had grown up on the island, Jo knew that Casey had known Lucy a lot longer than she had. Like most women, Lucy had a soft spot for him.

"I must be really bad if you two are here. I guess you're finally going to get me up in one of those helicopters," Lucy said. Her hands came up to touch her face, but Casey took the woman's small wrists and eased them back down. Lucy's hands had been burned badly, and Jo suspected the woman had gone into the kitchen to try to stop the fire herself and had received the burns in her efforts. "My face?"

"Still as pretty as ever," Casey said as he applied the electro pads for their monitors. The monitor began to alarm with an oxygen saturation reading in the eighties; he turned up the O2. "You're a smart lady. Putting the wet towel over your face was the best thing you could have done."

Lucy gave a muffled laugh against the oxygen mask, and then followed it up with a bout of coughing that wracked the woman's small frame.

Jo wanted to tell her that running from the fire instead of to the fire would have been the smart thing, but she'd wait until the woman was recovered to scold her.

"Call Dispatch and have them get us a receiving trauma hospital with a burn unit to transport to," Jo said to Roy via the radio hooked to her flight suit. Lucy was going to need some long-term care for the burns on her hands. Lucy loved to cook, and Jo hoped Lucy wouldn't lose the functionality she needed to run their busy pub.

Jo saw Casey motion to one of the EMTs as they began to strap Lucy onto the stretcher and she tried to speak, only the word *Darren* recognizable as she was overcome with another coughing spell.

"I'll call Darren as soon as we get you loaded up and headed to Miami," Casey said as they headed through the crowd with the people surrounding the scene moving quickly out of their way.

Jo saw that some of the onlookers began crying when they saw who was on their stretcher. Lucy was loved by so many people on the island.

"Wait," a man called from behind them as they exited the crowd and entered the area that the officers had cleared for their landing. "Casey. Jo."

Jo turned to see a man running up behind them, his long gray ponytail flapping against his back as he ran.

Recognizing the voice, Lucy tried to sit up, but the straps secured her in place.

"I'll talk to him," Casey told Lucy, walking back to where the man was being held back by officers. "Go ahead and load her up. I'll be right there."

By the time Roy had the all clear from the officers to start up, Casey had returned and they had Lucy hooked up to the monitors. As Jo began to radio the receiving hospital report, Casey got an IV started. Lucy needed the fluids as well as some pain medication.

"I gave Darren my cell phone number, and I'll call him as soon as we get you to the hospital," he told Lucy.

Jo watched as Lucy nodded. The fact that the woman wasn't trying to talk told Jo that Lucy's adrenaline rush was wearing off and now the extent of the situation was hitting her. A single tear slid down the woman's sooty cheek, clearing a path for what was sure to be more to come.

"It's going to be okay, Miss Lucy," Casey said. "Darren's headed to Miami right behind us."

"But my pub," Lucy said, the words so low that Jo read her lips more than heard them.

"You'll build it back. We'll help. Everyone will. Just rest right now," Jo said as Casey injected the IV port with some morphine.

Lucy's eyes closed and Jo watched as the tension eased from the woman's body, then another spell of coughing hit her.

The rest of the flight was silent, except for Lucy's coughing and the occasional beep of a monitor, until Roy gave them an ETA of five minutes.

Jo always thought of her job as a crazy mix of heartache and triumph. She had seen and experienced things that she never would have in any other profession. Some of it was good and some of it was not so good. Add to this the fact that the islands were small, it wasn't unusual for her to know one of their patients, which made it even harder for her and her coworkers when things ended badly. She'd had nightmares from some of the scenes she'd responded to and shed tears with coworkers over their losses and their wins. Today, she was going to count this one as a win. Lucy would have a lot of work ahead of her, but Casey had been right. They would all be there to help her.

That was just one of the things she loved about their island. One of the many reasons she was thankful that Casey had talked her into staying, even though their situation was awkward at times. They'd get through this and after Jeffrey left, things would get back to normal. She'd have her friends and her community and the job she loved.

She just wished she didn't have to keep reminding herself that things with Casey were just temporary. She told herself that soon they'd be back to their old friendship. But she was telling so many lies right now, letting people think she and Casey were romantically involved, that she wasn't sure if she could even believe herself.

# CHAPTER SIX

"IF SUMMER CALLS one more time, I am not answering the phone. She acts like we aren't capable of watching two babies," Jo said as she walked into the nursery where Casey sat in the middle of what looked like the aftermath of a hurricane.

"What happened?" she asked, unable to believe the tidy room she had left just minutes before could have been destroyed so fast.

"They ganged up on me," Casey said, from the floor where two eight-month-olds sat staring up at him, both faces angelic with their blond curls and big brown eyes.

"Sure they did," Jo said as she started picking up toys and putting them into the large toy box that had been emptied in record time.

"I was trying to figure out what they wanted to play with, but they don't seem to like any of their toys," Casey said as he wound up a toy car and sent it across the nursery floor while both the babies ignored it. "See."

"It seems they find you more fascinating," Jo said. Not that she could blame them. Dressed in jeans and a fitted black T-shirt, the man looked more like he was ready to hit the downtown clubs than babysit. She looked down at her own khaki shorts and the baggy novelty T-shirt she'd bought at a tourist stop in Miami, which was much more practical for the night ahead of them.

"Summer said they'd be getting hungry soon. Maybe we should change and feed them." Though the two babies didn't look hungry, they looked more puzzled by Casey's presence in their room. "I thought you had spent some time with the twins."

"I see them at work sometimes when Summer brings them in to see Alex," Casey said.

"But you like kids," Jo said as she bent over to pick up the little princess, Maggie, leaving the little prince, Jacob, for Casey.

"I like kids. These are not kids. Kids walk and talk. I don't know what to do with babies," Casey said, though Jo noticed he seemed very comfortable picking up the little boy.

"Don't you want kids someday?" Jo asked as they made their way to the kitchen.

Casey stopped and held the boy out at arm's length, studying him. "I don't know. I haven't given it much thought."

"It might be time for you to start thinking about it. You're not getting any younger, and you don't want to be one of those fathers that get mistaken for the child's grandfather." Though the thought of Casey becoming a father was hard to imagine. He'd have to find a woman to stick with longer than three months, something he hadn't done in all the time she had known him.

"I've got plenty of time. I'm not the one with the biological clock ticking. You should be worried about yourself," Casey said as he studied the buckle of the high chair that matched the one Jo was buckling Maggie into.

"My clock is doing just fine," Jo said, hearing the edge of anger in her voice. Her fertility had been discussed too many times when she'd been married to Jeffrey. He'd wanted to discuss the when, the where, even the how.

It had just been one more thing he wanted control over.

Now she had come to terms with the fact that she might not ever have children, but there was still a tender spot in her heart that throbbed at night when she was alone in bed. A part that ached for the happily-ever-after she'd been promised. The fact that it had turned into a nightmare instead should have taught her that the fairy tale of undying love was just that, a big fat lying tale. But still she dreamed of finding that love with someone, someday. That it was Casey who always played the part of the prince in those dreams was something she refused to acknowledge.

Casey gave her a questioning look, but she chose to ignore him as she prepared the food Summer had left for the babies. When Jacob began to fuss, she handed Casey a bowl with mashed sweet potatoes and a small spoon.

He studied the spoon and then began to feed the little boy. Maggie, seeing her brother getting fed before her, began to cry.

"See, this is what I mean," Casey said as he stopped and stared at the red-faced, crying little girl who had been an angel until then. "Kids don't do this. If one kid was eating and the other got tired of waiting for their turn, they'd just grab the other one's food."

"I'm sure that will happen in the future between these two, but right now crying is the only way they can tell you that they're not happy." Jo placed a spoonful of sweet potatoes in the crying girl's mouth. The silence that followed was priceless.

Her phone rang and she pulled it from her pocket. Maybe once Summer knew her children were being fed properly she'd relax and enjoy her night out. "They're eating their sweet potatoes and I've already cut up their bananas, so you can quit worrying. Me and Casey have this under control."

"Joanne? What are you talking about? And who is Casey?" Jeffrey asked, his voice so clear she looked around the room to make sure he wasn't standing in there with her.

Startled and cursing herself for not checking her caller ID before answering her phone, she couldn't answer him. When Casey took the phone from her hands, she didn't object. She knew that Alex and Summer had the best security that money could buy, but at that moment it did nothing to make her feel safe.

All she could think was that Jeffrey could be here, in Key West or even on Alex's property.

She looked over at the babies. No matter what, she wouldn't let him bring her friends and their children into this.

"Who is this?" Casey asked, though she was sure he knew exactly who it was just by her reaction.

With the roaring of the adrenaline rush in her ears, she couldn't hear whatever it was that Jeffrey said to Casey, but she didn't need to. There would be threats and bullying. It was how he handled everyone who did something he didn't like.

"I'm a friend," Casey said as he turned toward her and she met his eyes, "and her lover. And who are you?"

They both stood there a moment, then Casey held the phone out to her. Jeffrey had hung up.

"Well, that was short and sweet. I thought he'd have more questions for me. I guess he decided we couldn't be friends. And I was so looking forward to getting to know him better after the nice threats he issued if I didn't put you back on the phone."

"It's not funny," Jo said. "I don't even know

where he is. What if he's on the island? What if he tries to get in here?"

Casey handed her the phone before wrapping his arms around her. "I'm sorry. I know there is nothing funny about this situation. I should have thought to ask him where he was calling from, but I don't think he would have told me."

She sank into the warmth of him. His arms felt so good around her. She felt safe and treasured there. She let her own arms wrap around his waist, needing to feel closer to him. It was something she'd never felt free to do before. It was funny how fear could give you the strength to do things you normally wouldn't be brave enough to do. Resting her head against his chest, the soft cotton shirt against her cheek, she could hear the drum of his heart. So steady. Just like him. Never sputtering. Always constant. He was her rock right now.

And she couldn't take advantage of that by pretending what he felt for her was anything more than friendship, even though she wanted nothing more than to stand there in his arms, his body warm and hard against her own, forever. But she had to step away before her body did something that her brain knew would be a mistake.

"What the..." Casey said.

She tensed, afraid that he had somehow realized that it was desire that kept her in his arms instead of the need for comfort. Looking up, she saw that he was focused on where the twins sat quietly in their high chairs. It was the realization that they'd been a little too quiet that had her spinning out of his arms.

But the royal twins sat perfectly content. It didn't seem to bother them a bit that they were covered in the orange sweet potato that was supposed to have been their dinner.

"What do we do now?" Casey asked.

"We clean them up and start again," Jo said as she reached for a cloth, glad that there was something to do to keep her mind off Jeffrey's phone call. She had to find the strength to fight down the fear his voice automatically produced. She'd looked forward to tonight all week and now he'd ruined it. Hadn't he ruined enough of her life already? Why couldn't he just leave her alone?

Casey carefully laid the little boy down in his bed. The only babies he had ever cared for had been ones that were sick and, most of the time, fighting for their lives. He'd seen the faces of their parents and wondered how they endured the fear and the heartache of having a child who was suffering, or worse, one they were in danger of losing. But this little guy, dressed in the superhero sleeper Jo had let Casey pick out, was healthy and content. Babies had always seemed so fragile to him. But wasn't everyone at some point in their life, even after they grew up?

He looked over to where Jo sat in a rocking chair, holding the little princess. He'd seen the baby's eyes shut even before Jacob had fallen asleep in his own arms, but still Jo held her, the chair slowly moving backward and forward. They both knew that Jo was continuing to hold her more for her own comfort now than the baby's.

She'd been nervous throughout the night, jumping every time the air conditioner unit turned on or the wind rustled something outside. He'd reminded her that Alex's security system was state-of-the-art and monitored live by a company in California that would notify both Alex, the local police and whoever was in the house if there was a breach in their security. It didn't help. She was determined that she was putting everyone in danger by being there. What did she think her friends were going to do? Just stand by and let her ex-husband hurt her? They'd all stand up for her if they needed to.

He'd felt her body tremble against his, and it had scared him. He would have destroyed the man who had done that to her if he could have. But it seemed no matter how much he told her that he would keep her safe, she didn't believe him. She didn't trust him to protect her, and he needed to fix that or she was going to run.

Finally, she stood and placed the baby in her crib, though she stood there beside her for a few minutes before joining him at the door.

"I saw some pizza in the fridge we can heat up," Casey said as Jo followed him silently down the hall. "I'm starved. I didn't know babysitting could be such hard work."

"It's one of the parenting rules that you make sure you feed your babysitter. Summer was just so excited about a night out that she didn't think about it. I bet if I break into her secret stash of lobster bisque in the freezer she'll feed us better next time," Jo said.

"I'm okay with the pizza, but feel free to eat the bisque and give Summer a hard time. Not that I'm volunteering to do this on a regular basis." It had actually been a fun evening once the babies had warmed up to him. While Jo had taken on bath duty, he'd been assigned the duty of getting them dressed. It had reminded him of a wrestling match. One which he had won, as witnessed by the fully clothed babies asleep in their cribs.

As he heated up the pizza, Jo turned on the sound system, setting it to some mellow jazz, his favorite. They ate on the couch, him with his pizza and her with her soup, and talked about everything except what was on both of their minds. He could ignore this thing that hung between them, but that wasn't his way.

He believed in facing a problem head-on as he had done when he'd taken the phone and tried to get Jo's ex to talk to him. Had it agitated the man more? Oh, yeah. He'd hit home with his lie about being Jo's lover. Jeffrey was full of jealousy and rage right now. But it was at him, not Jo, which had been his intention. If Jo realized that had been his plan, Casey would be in trouble. Right now, though, he didn't have to worry about it. If or when Jeffrey showed up, Casey would deal with him man-to-man while assuring that Jo went unharmed. Until then, Casey's job was making sure Jo stayed put in Key West where he could keep her safe.

"Feeling better?" he asked. He needed to get Jo to talk to him. He wanted to find out where her head was.

"Some," she said. "I might have overreacted. And I know that you're right. Jeffrey isn't going to break in here tonight. Besides having great security, it isn't his way. He prefers to appear as the good guy. But what you did, telling him that we're lovers, I wish you hadn't. He'll see it as a challenge."

"Wasn't that the plan all along? That we let people think that we're lovers so that when he showed up he'd see that you've moved on and that I'm here with you. That I'm going to be there to protect you. That he can't have you back. Can't threaten you or hurt you anymore."

Casey's throat got tighter with each word. He felt like he'd been sitting on a keg of dynamite ready to explode ever since he'd gotten on the phone with Jo's ex. He'd known the man was worthless and a bully, but hearing his rants on the phone and the threats he'd made to him and Jo had given him a taste of what she had gone through in her marriage. No one should treat someone that way. Not man or woman.

"I know that's the plan. I agreed to it. But I have some second thoughts now. Besides, I'm not sure anyone is buying our act," Jo said.

"Why do you think that?" he asked.

"I don't know. It just seems that people would have their doubts. You have to admit that I'm not like the women you usually date."

"What? I have a type now?" he asked. With Key West being a popular international tourist spot, he'd dated a diverse group of women from all over the world. "I don't know why you would think that."

"Maybe because all your women are gorgeous. When's the last time you dated a plain Jane like me?"

Her question startled him and then made him mad. "Plain Jane? What does that even mean? There's nothing plain about you. Besides being smart and beautiful, both inside and out, you're too complicated for anyone to call you 'plain.'"

He put his pizza down and turned toward

her, taking her face in his hands. "When I see you, I see a caring woman who works hard every day to help others. A woman who would take time from her life to babysit for a friend. And a woman who has always been there when I needed her."

"That's not what I meant. I meant I don't look like the women you date."

"So you're saying that I think you're good enough to be my friend, but not good enough for me to date? Is that what you're saying?"

"No. Yes. I don't know," Jo said. She tried to turn away from him, but when he rested his forehead on hers, she stilled.

"I don't know who told you you're plain—" though he had a good idea "—but they were lying to you. You're beautiful, Jo. Men look at you all the time. I've told you that."

"And you growl at them," Jo said, her lips forming a saucy pout that had him forgetting what he had been saying.

"If that's all it takes to run them off, they don't deserve you. Any man would be proud to be seen with you. If it wasn't for you being my best friend, I'd ask you out and no man would scare me off." He stilled, realizing what he had just admitted.

Jo stared at him, her eyes wide as the tip of her tongue swept across her bottom lip.

He'd never noticed just how plump or how sexy her wide lips were until now. As if in a trance, he couldn't take his eyes off them. Before he knew what he was doing, he was moving in to taste them, a part of his brain going haywire as his lips were about to touch hers. A part he had tried to ignore for years had always wondered what it would be like to kiss Jo. Now he would know.

The front door suddenly opened, and they looked up to see Alex and Summer standing in the doorway staring at them.

"So, we leave you to babysit my angels and you end up making out. I am so disappointed in you two," Alex said, though there was a big smile plastered on his face.

For a moment he felt as if he had gotten caught making out on his parents' couch, something that might have happened a couple times in his high school days. Then, remembering that he and Jo needed everyone to believe they were a couple so that when Jeffrey showed up their story would be supported, he put his arm around Jo's shoulders and pulled her against him.

"I'm not disappointed," Summer said as she ducked under her husband's arm and came toward them. "I think it's wonderful. I just wish I'd taken a picture so I could post it around town. It's time everyone knows that the great Casanova of Key West is off the market."

Casey groaned loudly, getting the laugh from his friends that he had wanted. He wasn't sure what had just happened between him and Jo, but he knew that if they hadn't been interrupted they'd be doing exactly what his friends were accusing them of. He could still feel desire racing through his body with just the thought of his lips touching Jo's. Unable to help himself, he looked down at her. Oh, yes, those lips still looked way too kissable.

Her eyes met his, and he saw a hunger that matched his own. Where was this coming from? There had never been anything physical between them before. He'd always made sure of that. Friendship and romance didn't mix. He knew it, and he was sure Jo would agree with him.

Maybe they were just confused by this act they were playing. He knew his body sure seemed to be. Or maybe this was just a temporary thing that would pass by morning, leaving them laughing at what fools they'd been. But what if it didn't? What if he'd ruined everything by giving in to that one moment of desire?

The fact that he was still thinking about that almost-kiss, even now, after Summer and Alex had saved them from that danger, was not a good sign.

# CHAPTER SEVEN

Jo LIFTED THE bucket of smoked-damaged sheetrock and began the walk to the dumpster that had been delivered to Lucy's to help with the cleanup. While the block exterior walls were still standing, the old interior had to be cleared out so that a contractor could begin rebuilding it. It was hard work, but she was glad to do her part for her friend.

Besides, it gave her a good reason to get out of the house where Casey had been tiptoeing around her. What did he think she was going to do? Hold him down and kiss him so that she could finally find out what it felt like to have his lips on hers?

Okay, maybe she had given that a thought or two, but not seriously. Maybe she should just come out and tell him that he was safe around her. She'd made it this many years without attacking him. That should count for something.

"You okay, Jo?" Darren called out from the door.

She looked around and realized that she had been headed in the wrong direction. "Sorry, I wasn't paying attention."

While Lucy was still recovering from her burns and the smoke inhalation, Darren had arrived to be on hand to supervise for her. He was quick to answer everyone's questions on Lucy's recovery and pass on how grateful the woman was for all their help. By the time they had the dumpster half-full, he had set up a couple barbecue grills and the smell of steak and burgers cooking began to overtake the stench of the burned building.

She had just emptied the bucket and started back when a familiar Jeep pulled up. Moose jumped out and headed toward her as if he hadn't seen her in days.

"Whoa, Moose. Be careful or you'll end up with soot on you and you'll have to get a bath." Moose's ears went on alert, and his tail began to wag. Her dog loved being in water more than anything else.

"It looks like you've got a lot done," Casey

said as he joined them, his eyes going everywhere but to her.

She wasn't surprised to see him. He'd offered to come by after his work at the dog shelter was done. Jo knew it was mean and petty that she had hoped he would stay away. They could use his help. If only she could get over this awkward feeling around him. This feeling that he knew she was looking at him while at the same time, she somehow knew he was looking back at her. They had danced around each other like this for two days now, and it was getting old. The tension between them was becoming unbearable. Was it so terrible that he had almost kissed her?

"We need to talk," she said, unable to go another minute without dealing with this invisible wall that had come up between them. They'd never had this awkwardness between them, and she didn't know how to handle it.

"About what?" Casey asked, finally looking at her before glancing away. He looked down at his feet then shuffled them around. She'd seen this before. It was the telltale sign that he wanted to be anywhere but where he was right now, which shouldn't have been the case. What did he see when he looked at her that was making him avoid her like this? She was the same old Jo she had always been. Was it so strange, so out of nowhere, that he recognized her as a woman? A woman that he'd almost kissed?

She thought about doing it. Just kissing him, right then and there, beside an old rusted dumpster so that she could get it over with. Maybe neither of them would like it. Maybe Casey would laugh and forget about it and life would go back to normal. At least for him.

Only she wasn't sure she wanted it to go back the way it was. She was tired of ignoring how she felt. She was tired of denying the attraction she had for him. An attraction that would be more than apparent if she did ever kiss the man, something that she didn't want to get into right then. Not the time. Not the place.

She turned to walk away. She'd just leave him there to stare off into space like he was doing right then. How long would it take him to notice that she was gone? A minute? Five?

"Food's ready," Darren called over the noise of the hammering and scraping going on in the pub.

"Just forget it," she said as she started toward where the rest of the crowd was headed. When a hand touched her shoulder, stopping her, she turned back to Casey, shocked to see the look of desire in his eyes.

"We promised not to mess things up between us," he said, reminding her of the vow she had insisted he make that night on the beach.

"I know," she said. "I just didn't know it was going to be this hard."

"Me either. You're important to me, Jo. Our friendship is important to me."

She didn't know what to say. Was it possible that she was reading Casey all wrong? Maybe it had just been her imagination. Maybe he had never even thought of kissing her.

Which would mean what? That she was the one causing all the tension in the relationship? If so, this would be even more awkward for her. How could she fix this?

"Our friendship is important to me too. I would never do anything to risk it. You know that." She spoke the truth; she just needed to remember it herself.

"I don't want things to change between us," Casey said as he bent down and picked up a piece of wood that had fallen from someone's pile of debris on its way to the dumpster.

The finality of his voice told her everything she needed to know. Maybe Casey had started to kiss her, but he wasn't happy about it. And he wasn't planning on repeating it. Which left her only one choice. She had to accept what he was saying now and his reasons for it so that this awkwardness between them could go away.

"Hey, you two," one of the EMTs said as he walked past them with a bucket of soggy Sheetrock, "you need to see this. It looks like we're about to get busy."

"We're both off today," Casey said as they followed the man to where Darren was serving food.

"Me too," the man said. "We better enjoy it while we can."

They grabbed some burgers and drinks then joined the crowd that surrounded the small television Darren had set up to watch the college football games. Only it wasn't football they were all watching. Instead, on the screen a picture of deep blue water showed a red swirl moving through the Atlantic. When the weather forecaster drew lines from the tropical system, which had just been named Ileen, up to Florida with more than one line crossing close to the Keys, they all groaned. She was using words like sheering and fronts, but all Jo saw were the spaghetti models that showed the storm headed straight for them.

"It's only a tropical depression," Jo said, trying to find some hope for the group, which was made up mostly of first responders. "Maybe it will only bring us some rain."

"It's rained all summer. We don't need anymore," one of them said while another groaned in the background. "I'm tired of rain."

"But the winds are already at forty-five miles per hour," another one said.

"I hope Lucy isn't watching this," Darren said from behind them. "She'll worry even more about this place."

"Then we better get back to work and get the pub boarded up before she breaks out of the hospital and heads down here," Casey said, getting another groan from the group as the television returned to the football game that was in progress.

"Do we need to be worried?" Jo asked

Casey, watching as the others filed past them back into the burned-out interior of the building.

"No. We've weathered storms before. We'll make it through this one too," he said, giving her a smile that she hadn't seen since the night they'd babysat the twins.

Jo stopped and stared at him as he followed the others into the soot-covered entrance, a big shovel slung over his shoulder. Was he talking about the weather or their turbulent relationship? Either way, she knew a storm was coming, and she didn't share his optimism. All storms were dangerous. They could hurt and destroy. The only thing she could do now was to hope that the two of them and their friendship were strong enough to get through it.

When Casey's phone went off the next morning, he wasn't surprised. He'd closed down the bar with some of the other EMTs, and they'd all made a point to keep up with the weather updates during the evening. The higher the winds got, the more somber the crowd became. By the time he'd headed home, the winds had reached seventy-five miles an hour and Tropical Storm Ileen had gotten an upgrade to Hurrican Ileen. Only the timing of a low front would decide whether the islands would be impacted.

"We've got an hour to report to headquarters," Jo called from below the stairs.

He grunted something he hoped sounded like "okay" then rolled onto his back and stared at the ceiling. He should have headed home when Jo had. He wasn't one for staying out all night. He spent so many nights working that he had learned to appreciate a night of good sleep. But last night, when Jo had left, he found himself holding back. He wasn't even sure why. All he knew was once Jo had checked in and let him know she'd made it home safely, the tension he'd felt for the last few days finally subsided.

What he didn't want to admit, even to himself, was that without Jo around he could finally relax. He didn't need to be on constant alert. He didn't need to look away whenever he caught a glimpse of those tempting lips that had almost got them in trouble. He didn't need to leave the room when the atmosphere began to hum with a sexual tension that he had never experienced before. There at the bar, he could nurse a beer and think of nothing more dangerous than the threatening storm that seemed intent to visit the Keys.

"I'm putting on some coffee and making some eggs and toast. Do you want some?" Jo called, her voice nearer now.

He looked over from his loft bed to see her standing on the ladder. Her hair was wet from her shower, but she had already dressed for the day in a pair of fitted jeans and a pink-striped shirt. His body reacted like it was a force of nature, becoming hard and demanding. He fought against a groan that was instinctive. All he wanted right then was to pull the sheets back over his head and go back to sleep. Not that he wanted to return to his dreams. The erotic picture of Jo spread out on his bed, this bed, was part of the reason he was in trouble right then. The only safe thing he could do was remain where he was and find a way to get rid of her.

"Coffee sounds amazing, but I'd really love some bacon with those eggs and toast. And maybe instead of eggs you could make it a cheese omelet? And there's some onion and tomatoes you can add too." He felt bad for asking her to do more work, but it would keep her busy. And it would give him and his traitorous body time to recover.

"Okay, but you better hurry. We don't have a lot of time," she said as her head disappeared from the landing and she headed back down the stairs.

Once in the shower, he didn't want to leave. His world was complicated with problems he had never imagined, and he'd rather cower in the shower than face what was waiting in the kitchen. But that wasn't possible. He only had a few minutes to eat and get to work. After the water was turned off, the smell of frying bacon drifted over the steamy bathroom. Unable to help himself, he quickly dressed and followed the smell into the kitchen, only to find it empty with the plate of food waiting on the stove for him.

There was no Jo waiting there to ask a million questions about what he thought of their bosses' request for all staff to report for a mandatory meeting. No Jo to drill him on the possible damage Hurricane Ileen could do if she hit the islands. No Jo to tell him all about what was trending on her news feed.

No Jo to smile at him from across the table. And instead of feeling free, he felt disappointed. Which didn't make any sense at all. He'd been the one to tell Jo that he didn't want their relationship to change, that he wanted their lives to go back to the way they were before they had started all of this pretending. He'd always liked his quiet mornings in his home before Jo had moved in. What was wrong with him?

Unable to sit there, alone, any longer, he poured his coffee in a mug and made a sandwich from the toast, eggs and bacon. He told himself it was because he didn't have the time to eat. He tried to believe it.

When he arrived at work, he was surprised to see so many people. Every chair in the building had been rounded up and there were still people standing. There were the nurses and paramedics that he worked with, and the three pilots who rotated in and out of duty. But there were a couple others he didn't recognize.

"Who are the suits?" he asked as he took a place next to Dylan, Alex's assistant and one of the best flight paramedics Casey had ever known.

"They're from the county emergency services and the tourist council. They just finished a meeting with Alex. He must have invited them to stay, probably so we can ask any questions." They both moved over as Katie, Dylan's wife, joined them.

Casey looked through the crowd and saw that Jo was sitting up front. As he looked, she turned and waved. He started to wave back then realized it was Katie she was motioning to.

"Jo and Summer saved me a seat in the front. Do you mind?" Katie asked Dylan.

"Of course not. I'll see you after the meeting," Dylan said, before dropping a kiss on his wife's upturned face.

"Lunch at Marco's?" she asked.

"That sounds perfect," Dylan said.

Casey watched as Katie made her way to the front, where she was quickly surrounded by her friends. When he looked over at Dylan, he saw that he was also watching his wife.

"Don't the two of you ever get tired of spending so much time together?" Casey asked, only realizing too late that his mouth had voiced what his brain had been wondering.

"Me and Katie?" Dylan asked. "Of course

not. Why? Are you already getting tired of having Jo around all the time?"

"I guess everyone knows she's staying with me?" Casey asked. Not that he was surprised. Though there were easily fifteen people at the meeting, they were still a tight crew.

"Staying with you?" Dylan asked. "Don't you mean she's moved in with you?"

Casey didn't see the difference, but he nodded. "It's all kind of new. I'm just trying to figure it out as I go."

"Says the man who swore he'd always remain a bachelor," Dylan said.

"It wasn't so long ago that you were saying the same thing," Casey said. But Katie had barely arrived on the island when Dylan had fallen for her. "And I'm still a bachelor. We haven't made any long-term plans."

"The two of you have been headed this way for years. You just didn't know it," Dylan said.

Casey started to ask what he meant, but Alex had made his way to the front of the room. Everyone paused their conversations, as all of them were anxious to hear why they had been called in.

"Thanks everyone for coming," Alex said. "I'm sure by now you are all aware that there is a storm out in the Atlantic. The National Hurricane Service is watching this one closely as it has become more organized overnight. Mr. Dean is here from Monroe County Emergency Services and had asked that I hold this meeting on the chance that the Keys are impacted. As we all know, these storms can be unpredictable, but we need to be prepared."

As Alex stepped back, one of the men in a dark suit came forward. "As your boss was saying, these storms can change quickly and here on the Keys we want to be ready. If it's determined that Hurricane Ileen will threaten the Keys, a mandatory evacuation order will be issued asking all visitors to leave. If this happens, the county tourist development council will advise those visitors on the evacuation. That decision would be made by emergency services, hopefully twenty-four hours before impact."

As Casey listened, the man went into the necessary bridge closings due to winds, evacuation of locals, and finally, why they had all been called in—the possibility of needing to evacuate patients from the local hospital.

"We've been here before. We prepare for the worst and hope for the best. But Hurricane Irma taught us that though we don't get hit often, the Keys are as vulnerable as the rest of the state of Florida. We want to have a plan in place in case the worst happens."

The man stepped back and Alex stepped forward. "I'll be sending out emails to each one of you with a plan and schedule for evacuations if it becomes necessary. If Hurricane Ileen does decide to make a visit here, we will be prepared. I ask that you stay in touch and prepare your families and stay safe."

As soon as Alex stepped back, everyone seemed to talk at once. If the local emergency services issued an evacuation order, it would be all hands on deck. There wouldn't be time for the first responders to get their own homes ready for the storm, and they all knew it.

The small cottage that was his home had been entrusted to him by his grandmother, and he took the responsibility to protect it seriously. He checked the weather app on his phone and saw that the winds had increased. Eighty miles an hour. Still a Category 1.

"What's up?" Jo said, from beside him.

Startled, he looked down to see that most of the room had cleared out. It looked like everyone had the same thought that he did. Time to prepare. "How do you feel about helping me hang some hurricane shutters?"

"I can't think of anything I'd rather do," Jo said.

And just like that everything seemed right between them.

# CHAPTER EIGHT

"ONLY ONE MORE to go," Jo said as she climbed down from the ladder. Her back was killing her and her arms had begun to shake with the weight of the metal hurricane shutters, but it was good, hard work and it was just what she needed right then. There was no worrying about Jeffrey, Casey or the hurricane while you were up on an eight-foot ladder stretching for every inch while supporting your side of a heavy metal shutter.

Her phone went off with an update from her weather app as she reached the last step. It looked like Hurricane Ileen was not in a hurry to share her destination as she spun around the Atlantic at a crawl.

"Any change?" Casey asked as he came off his own ladder.

His T-shirt was plastered against his chest with sweat, but somehow he still looked good.

Meanwhile, she was sporting a pair of unde
arm sweat rings, and the hair she'd knotte
on the top of her head had come loose an
hung limp from the smothering humidity.
was so unfair.

"The winds have increased to eighty-fiv
miles an hour but no change in direction. Cu
ba's talking about evacuation orders now."

"If it doesn't change in the next few hour
we'll be sending out our own evacuation o.
ders. Then the real work will begin. Peopl
will panic trying to leave the Keys, and we'
be flooded with wrecks on Highway 1 an
boating accidents in the Gulf," Casey sai
"Thanks for the help here."

They both looked back at the house. J
knew how much it had meant to Casey whe
his grandmother had willed it to him. It ha
stood up to many storms throughout its life
time, but somehow they both knew this wa
different.

"It'll be okay," she said, though she sti
worried.

"I hope so. And now that we've done all w
can here, what about your place?" Casey sai

Her place? She hadn't even thought of he
apartment. It had only been a few days sin

she'd moved into Casey's place, and she had almost forgotten the little apartment she had called home.

"My landlord will take care of boarding up the windows, if it comes to that. I should probably go over and check things out though." She'd packed up her books, personal papers and pictures to take with her when she had planned to leave the island, but she hadn't brought them with her to Casey's. She needed to make sure they would be safe. "It won't take but a moment though. I don't have that much there to worry about."

Casey's phone dinged with a message, and he pulled it out. "Roy says a bunch of the EMTs are getting together tonight at the tiki bar. Want to go?"

"Sure. I'll drive my car and stop by my place on the way." It could be a long time before any of them got a chance to get together if Hurricane Ileen didn't decide to take a detour.

"Maybe I should go with you," Casey said as they headed indoors to clean up.

"I'll be fine. It'll only take a moment, and even Jeffrey is smart enough to not visit an island that has a hurricane headed its way.

I'll have my phone with me in case there's a problem."

"Okay, but call me if anything doesn't feel right. I'll only be a few minutes away," Casey said.

"Come on, Moose, let's go get cleaned up and put on our party clothes," she called to the dog who'd been giving them moral support by barking at each and every car that had passed the house as they'd worked.

By the time Jo and Moose headed to her apartment, the sun was starting to set. She was relieved to see that the landlord had begun the process of nailing the large sheets of plywood across the windows of the apartments. There were still some windows where supplies had been stacked for work to resume the next day, but all of the windows of her own apartment that she could see from the parking lot had been covered.

But as she opened the door to her apartment, she hesitated. With no light from the windows, the room was darker than a moonless night sky. There was none of the warmth of the home she had known for the last four years. Instead, it seemed abandoned and lonely. Moose whined from beside her and her hand went down to pat his head.

"It's okay. We just need to turn the lights on," she told him, then flipped the switch that flooded the room with a stark white illumination. "See, Moose. Everything is okay."

Still chilled from the eerie atmosphere, Jo went through each room turning on the lights. When the last room had been explored by both her and Moose, her nerves finally settled. "This is ridiculous," she told him. "We have a party to get to."

Not sure where the safest place for her treasured belongings would be, Casey had offered to keep them at his place inside an interior storage room and she'd agreed. His home had withstood hurricanes for generations. It was out of the usual flood zones and about as safe as she could ask for.

She'd just finished loading her last box when George, her neighbor, drove up.

"Are you coming or going?" he asked as he got out of his car.

"I just stopped by for a few things," Jo said. They'd been neighbors for as long as she'd lived there, exchanging pleasantries and gossip about other renters as they came and went. He'd always been nice, and she'd felt safe knowing he was living beside her. More than once he'd helped with small projects around her place, and she'd always returned the favor by taking care of his cat, Flo, when he'd headed to Miami to visit his parents.

"I'm glad to see they've got most of the windows boarded up," she said.

"Yeah, they started late, but maintenance says they'll have it finished by noon tomorrow. I'm packing up me and Flo tonight and going to stay with my parents. Hopefully I'm just being cautious, but it will make my parents feel better. My dad even agreed to let Flo stay."

She knew George's dad had terrible allergy issues, so his agreeing to host Flo as well as George was a sign that people were beginning to take this storm seriously. "I think that sounds like a good idea."

"Oh, yeah. I've got a package that was delivered a few days ago. I had told one of your friends, the one that's some kind of royalty. I recognized her from the TV. She seemed real nice too. I'll go get it for you."

Jo remembered that Summer had said something about a package, but as Jo hadn't ordered anything online recently, she hadn't given it another thought. It was probably something from her parents.

She waited while George opened his door then returned with a long rectangle package.

"Here it is," he said, handing it to her.

It was wrapped in brown paper and didn't weigh much. She tried again to recall anything she might have ordered, but there was nothing. Then she saw the address from the sender. Written in a thin cursive that she would recognize anywhere, Jeffrey had scrolled his name and address.

Something skittered up her spine, a foreboding or a premonition, she wasn't sure what it was, but it wasn't good. It sent her on alert and her eyes scanned the parking lot, looking for any sign of her ex-husband. But there was nothing. She recognized the few cars in the lot as belonging to other renters. Besides, this package had been delivered days before.

She remembered the call she'd received from her ex-husband while she and Casey had been babysitting. Was that why he had called? To see if she had received this package?

"Thanks, for keeping this for me," she said,

though every inch of her body wanted to re-coil from the box.

"No problem. I've got to get packed, but you stay safe up there in the skies while I'm gone," George said, before heading back into his apartment.

Jo tightened her hand on Moose's leash as she made her way back to her car. She loaded Moose then laid the box on the seat beside her before shutting the car door. She didn't want to open it. Not now. She'd been look-ing forward to sharing the next few hours with Casey and the rest of their friends. She'd dressed in a short, fitted, pale blue dress that screamed to be let out onto the dance floor. And now all her excitement for the night had vanished.

Knowing that waiting to open the package would only make this worse, she picked the box up and read Jeffrey's address again. It was the same one they had shared once upon a time. It was supposed to have been their for-ever home. The one they would raise a family in someday. It had been none of those things, at least not for her. She hadn't even blinked when he insisted on keeping the house in their divorce settlement. She'd wanted nothing that she had shared with him.

Pulling the brown paper from the package, she found a white floral box underneath. The cloying smell of wilted red roses seeped from the box before she lifted the lid. Inside there was a note, one of those small rectangle cards that were provided by the florist. As she read the words, her hands began to shake.

She shut the box carefully then set it to the side. Cranking her car, she rolled down her window as she started down the road. The warm air, heavy with late summer humidity, did nothing to cool the anger that was beginning to boil through her veins.

Yes, she'd made mistakes. She should have been stronger. She should have seen Jeffrey for who he really was instead of the charming prince he had made himself out to be, but how long would she have to pay for her mistakes? What was it about her that had screamed victim to him? She'd been an independent woman before he had come into her life. Why couldn't he just accept that she had moved on with her life and leave her to it?

He'd made her leave her home. He'd taken away the safety she'd always felt in her new life. Now, when she'd made friends that were more like family, he was trying to take all that away from her by scaring her into running. Why did he have to spoil all of that?

Casey had been right when he'd told her she couldn't run away again. She'd left her hometown and Jeffrey still hadn't forgotten about her. She hadn't even been home to see her parents since the day she'd packed her little car and headed as far south as it was possible to go.

She pulled into the small parking lot and her eyes immediately went to where Casey's truck sat. She needed him. She needed to know he was near. Know he would keep her safe. Know that someone cared about her even though she was bringing them into a situation that was all her fault. She just needed Casey to put his warm arms around her and make the awful coldness that had seeped into her bones go away.

Jo saw him the moment she walked up to the open-air bar, and she froze. Standing by Casey, her hand resting against his chest as she spoke, stood Sarah. Something broke inside of Jo. It wasn't her heart. She'd built too many barriers around it where Casey was concerned. Instead, it was this buildup of anger, this boiling cauldron of every pain and fear and the resulting fury that she'd repressed over the last five years that had finally broken free. Anger at Jeffrey for destroying the safe life she had made for herself on the islands. Anger at herself for putting up with the way he had treated her when they were married. And a new anger, one directed at Casey for letting this woman touch him when, at least to the rest of the world, he was supposed to be loyal to her.

Before she knew it, she found herself across the room and pushing between the two of them. As Sarah protested with a shriek that could be heard from across the crowd, Jo turned to Casey.

Driven by the anger, the hurt and a stupid feeling of betrayal that she had no right to feel, Jo turned away from Sarah and grabbed the collar of Casey's shirt, pulling his head down till his face was even with hers. Laughing blue eyes met hers, and it only made her madder.

"You think this is funny?" she asked. His lips parted in a grin that answered her question. Was he laughing at her? Really? She'd just saved the man from his troubled ex and he just thought it was a game. But wasn't his whole life a game? He played women like they were instruments then moved on when one of them wanted more than to be a playmate. Well, if he liked games, she would be happy to play one with him. Let him see how he liked it.

She pulled his face closer and before he could realize what she was going to do, she crushed his lips against hers. It wasn't a fun kiss or a friendly kiss. No. This was a kiss meant to conquer, and she poured into it every bit of frustration she'd ever had while watching this man kiss another woman.

When he didn't pull back, she let go of his collar and wrapped her arms around his neck as she pressed her body even closer to his. Her breasts rubbed against his chest, and her nipples tightened to painful peaks. A heat she'd forgotten existed lit down in the pit of her core and exploded outward until her whole body seemed on fire. Her lips parted against his, and it was only when his tongue swept inside, tangling with hers, that she discovered she wasn't the only one being drawn into this dance of need and want.

His hands clasp her bottom and lifted her, turning her until she found herself pressed against something hard and rough against her back. Her hands tangled in Casey's blond curls and his hands pressed her even closer, the hard length of him imprinted against her body.

It was only when someone yelled, "Get a room!" from across the noisy bar that Jo's overheated brain began to surface and take control from a body that wanted nothing more than to finish what Jo had so stupidly started in a room filled with people she'd have to face later.

The thought of the smiles and winks she would receive from more than one nameless EMT after this stunt sobered her instantly. She'd made a fool of herself in front of everyone. And Casey? He probably thought she was putting on a show for Sarah and the crowd just to convince them that he and Jo were involved.

For a second she buried her face in Casey's shoulder. She couldn't face him. Couldn't face anyone. She didn't even want to face herself.

She pushed away and started for the restroom, then turned at the last minute to the steps that led down to the beach. Jo could still hear Sarah's voice, raised in anger at Casey, when she made it down to the bottom step. Kicking off her shoes, she began to run down the beach, only discovering that Moose ran beside her when she heard his panting.

She ran until the only sound she could hear was the waves crashing against the shoreline. Now panting herself, she stumbled then tripped on her feet and tumbled into the sand.

She lay there doing nothing, feeling nothing. The fear, the anger, the need; they were gone now, washed away as the rhythmic waves rushed in and out. She was only numb. Just numb. She couldn't even cry, though she wanted to. A good, cleansing cry, as her mother had always called it, helped set things right sometimes. But she didn't have it in her.

It was shock. That had to be it. She'd gone from one emotion to another too close together, and her body couldn't handle it. She rested her overheated cheek against the cool sand and closed her eyes. She was tired and wrung out. She'd just rest a few minutes, then she'd get herself up and march back to that bar and face whatever she had to face. But not now. Not yet. Now she just wanted to be alone and to rest.

Casey looked up and down the beach. Though not yet full, the moon was on the increase, brightly reflecting against the water. Where had Jo gone? By the time he'd managed to get rid of Sarah and her accusations that he had lied to her about his feelings for Jo, there had been no sign of her. He didn't like the thought of her out alone on the beach at night, though he knew Moose would be able to protect her from most dangers.

As if on cue, Casey spotted the Great Dane to his right, loping down the beach toward him. He waited a moment, expecting Jo to be lagging behind the long-legged dog, but there was no sign of her.

"Where's Jo, Moose?"

The dog sprinted around him circling once, then twice, spraying sand as his paws dug into the ground. Then just as suddenly as he had come, he headed back down the beach.

"I guess that means I'm supposed to follow him," Casey said to himself as he took off at a jog.

He'd almost given up on reaching Moose when he spotted him at the top of the beach. Beside him sat Jo, one arm around the big dog. His breath came a little easier now that he could see that she was safe.

But now that he had found her, he didn't really know what he would say to her. It seemed like they had said everything there was to say with that kiss they had just shared. Where did they go from here? It was all good for them to play at being more than friends, but that kiss hadn't been an act. It had been hot and fresh and more than a little decadent. And now they had to face the reality that there was more, at least physically, between them besides friendship.

But it was the last thing he wanted. He didn't want to mess things up with Jo; he treasured their friendship too much. And while there were a few women he'd been able to remain friends with after their relationship had run its course, Jo was different. She'd been hurt by that rotten ex-husband of hers, and she deserved better than that. She deserved a man who understood how to treat her. He wasn't that man. He'd never been that man for anyone. He knew that.

He took life one day at a time with no worries about a future. Free and simple, that was the life he'd lived for years, and he didn't know if he could change. He didn't know if he wanted to. It was safe to live the way he did with no chance of being hurt by someone you trusted. He'd once planned a future with a woman, and then she'd walked away with someone else stating that what they'd had wasn't really love. It was just a friendship they'd mistaken for love.

If it hadn't been love he'd felt for Anna, what had it been?

He'd thought then that he'd never get over her. He'd been stupid and done things that had almost got him kicked out of the coast guard because the military didn't care how bad your heart was broken when you didn't show up for duty. He'd also learned that trying to drink your troubles away never worked. You just ended up with more trouble. Then his captain had called him into his office and given him some advice. Instead of worrying about falling in love with a woman, he just needed to concentrate on his job and if a woman got in the way of that job, he needed to stay away from them. Sure, it was okay to date women for fun, but he had to put the coast guard first. With that advice, he'd changed his lifestyle and priorities.

And when he'd left the coast guard, he carried that advice with him. Getting over his fiancée leaving him had taught him what was really important in life. Someone you thought cared for you could let you down, but your job and coworkers were always there for you. He liked to think he'd become a better man because of the experience, but that didn't mean he ever wanted to live through it again. And none of that was going to help him with the situation he was in with Jo.

*Because there had never been another Jo for you.*

And that scared him more than the kiss the two had shared.

Climbing up on the sandy hill, he took a seat, leaving Moose between them. They sat there with only the sound of the waves and an occasional car off in the distance. Silence had always been something that they were comfortable with, neither of them feeling the need to fill it with unnecessary chatter when they were together.

"I'm so sorry," Jo said, the words just above a whisper. "I don't know what happened."

Casey could describe in detail everything that had happened from the moment her soft, but demanding lips had had touched his to the moment she'd pulled away, leaving him hard and desperate and unable to focus on anything but the fact that she'd walked away from him without even a backward glance.

It had taken him a few minutes to understand that it had been the cheering crowd that had startled her into breaking whatever had taken hold of them. Only once he'd understood that she'd probably been embarrassed by the attention and had wanted to get away from the crowd, not running away from him, had he been able to clear his mind and deal with the nonsense Sarah had been saying about him not being honest with her about his feelings for Jo.

"There's nothing to apologize for," he said. At least not on her part. He had been the one who had lost control, pushing her back against the hard wooden railing that encircled the bar's deck and plastering his body against hers. Just the memory of her body, so soft and responsive as it moved against him, had him rock hard in an instant.

"I embarrassed you," she said, her voice a little stronger now, though her eyes never strayed from the ocean waters that seemed to go on forever.

"Are you kidding me? I got more back-slaps from the guys than I got the day I delivered that baby in the back of the tour bus." It had been the highlight of his career for many years now.

"They must think I'm demented, jumping you like that," she said, then laughed. "Did you see Sarah's face? I was afraid she was having some sort of seizure."

"And you left me to deal with her alone," he said. He took a breath and let himself relax just a bit. Jo laughing he could deal with. "And no one thinks you're demented. We're supposed to be together. A couple. Couples kiss. Do you have any idea how many of those guys would like to have been in my place?"

"Why would you say that?" she asked.

The woman really had no idea how many heads turned when she entered a room.

"I said it, because it's true. Men look at you all the time." And he'd never liked it. "Some have even tried to ask you out, but you always seem to be able to dodge them."

"Maybe I'm waiting for Prince Charming so I can be a princess like Summer and…" She stopped. "No, I take that back. I married someone I thought was Prince Charming, and he turned out to be a frog in disguise. I have no desire to kiss another frog in my lifetime."

And just like that they were back to the subject of kissing.

Jo took a deep breath and finally looked at him. "I guess we need to talk about it."

"I guess we do." He knew she was right, though he had no idea what to say.

"Your place or mine?" she asked, before winking at him.

Was she serious? Or was she just joking with him as she tried to lighten the mood? A certain part of him hoped she wasn't joking. His brain, on the other hand, wasn't sure what to think. "Are you serious?"

"I don't know," she said. "What do you think we should do? Pretend it never happened?"

"That would be the easiest thing to do, wouldn't it?" he asked, though he didn't believe for one moment that it would work. A peck on the lips they could have ignored. What they'd shared had been much more than a kiss. It had been a whole-body experience, from lips to hips. If he'd found it hard to be around Jo after their almost-kiss at Alex and Summer's place, how was he supposed to ignore what they'd shared tonight? Things were just going to get worse between them if they didn't deal with this now.

"Maybe it was just a fluke," Jo said. Her eyes met his and held this time. "Maybe it was just the timing or something."

Did she really believe that? Something in her eyes told him that she didn't mean a word she was saying. So what was she after? "How do you suggest we find out?"

"I guess we could repeat it. Like an experiment. If nothing happens, we can laugh about it and move on, right?" Jo said as her hand came up and stroked Moose's neck.

It would be crazy to go along with this. His body was still recovering from just thinking about that kiss. But what if she was right? What if it had just been a one-time thing? Jo had always been off his sexual radar due to their friendship. Maybe all it had been was the temptation of forbidden fruit that had caused him to react so strongly.

"Okay. I'm game. When and where?" he asked, suddenly nervous and excited all at the same time. He didn't have to check his pulse to know that his heart was beating too fast; he could feel it trying to come out of his chest.

"How about now? Right here?" Jo said with a voice that showed none of the nervousness he was feeling, though he noticed she held Moose's collar in a death grip.

"Okay. Let's do it," he said with a fearlessness he didn't feel. "Are we going to try this with Moose between us?"

"Down, Moose," she ordered.

They both watched the big dog as he jumped down the hill in one big leap. The empty space Moose left between them was like a large gully that one of them had to cross. Neither made a move.

# CHAPTER NINE

Jo STARED AT the space between them. What had she been thinking to suggest this? That this was their one chance to find out if there was something more between them? And if there was? Casey had made no secret of the fact that he didn't want anything but her friendship. He was like an old man so set in his ways that no one was going to change him. He didn't want a permanent lover. He didn't want to be anything but a friend to her. He didn't want to accept that the passion in the kiss they'd shared had been real. But what about what she wanted?

She slid into the space between them and stopped. She had made the first move and now it was up to him. Jo needed to know that he wanted to see this through. If the kiss fizzled, she'd accept that it had been only her imagination that had dreamed up Casey's response to her. And if the two of them went up in flames like they had at the bar?

"It's your move," she said. "If you don't want to take it, I'll understand."

"And if I do?" he asked, his voice so deep and rough that it sent goose bumps over her bare skin.

She looked up from where she had been studying the empty beach to find him bending over her. She clenched her hands, willing them to remain by her side when all she wanted to do was wrap them around his neck and pull him closer. His firm lips softly stroked hers, and for a moment she thought that was all he intended. Then his tongue was licking its way inside her mouth and everything inside of her gave way to her body's instinctual need for him as she arched her body up toward his. She'd always known it would be like this between them.

Her hands found their way up his chest until they encircled his neck while she tried to remind herself that they were only sharing a kiss. Nothing more. Just one kiss.

One kiss that seemed to go on and on in a never-ending pleasure that she had never experienced before as he kissed her with a wickedly, wild tongue that stroked a fire deep inside of her. That flame spread up her chest and across her breasts, causing her nipples to harden.

Just a kiss? There was no such thing when she was in Casey's arms.

And it made her desperate for more. She wanted him closer. She wanted the clothes between them gone. She wanted him inside her with a need she'd never known for another man.

As if he could read her mind, Casey pulled his lips from hers and quickly moved away, leaving her head spinning and her body disoriented. It was as if she'd been climbing some tall mountain and suddenly everything that had kept her safe was gone. Slowly, she returned to the reality the two of them shared. One that she couldn't help but question now. Just why was it so wrong that they enjoyed each other like this? People did it all the time.

But Casey wasn't like other people. He didn't want to blur that line between friends and lovers. She looked up to see him staring at her like he'd been struck by lightning. The fact that she could hear him breathing in quick ragged breaths gave her some hope. She wasn't the only one who had felt the force of that kiss. He had to see there was something more than friendship between them now.

"So do we call this experiment a failure or a success?" she asked. It wasn't the question she wanted to ask. She wanted to ask why they had waited so long before doing this and how was she supposed to forget it now that they had?

"I don't know," Casey said, still staring at her like he'd never seen her before.

"Does that mean we need to do it again? Two out of three or something?" she asked, though as far as she was concerned the first two had been very successful.

Casey cleared his voice then looked away from her. "No, I think we can both agree that it wouldn't be a good idea to try that again."

Not knowing what else to say, she leaned back against the bank of sand and stared up at the stars. There were so many questions she wanted to ask, but every one of them seemed to lead back to what it was that prevented Casey from letting a woman inside those walls he'd built around his heart. He didn't talk about it much, but she knew it had to have something to do with the fiancée who, according to rumors, had left him at the altar.

"Do you ever wonder what would have happened if your fiancée had gone through with the wedding?" she asked. She was letting her subconscious take over her mouth tonight, and it didn't seem to care what came out. "I'm sorry. That was rude."

"It's okay. I was angry with you about not telling me about Jeffrey. It's only right that you get to ask me about Anna." He leaned back beside her, though she noticed he left plenty of room between them.

Would it always be like this between them now? Him, afraid to get too close to her, while she yearned for the feel of him next to her?

"I can't say I've considered what it would be like if we had married. When she left town with someone else, it was the end of things. What I thought we had together hadn't really existed according to her."

"But don't you ever wonder what marriage to her, or to someone you loved would be like? I know my marriage was a nightmare, but that doesn't mean I think they all are."

"No. I don't. She decided that we had mistaken our friendship for love. End of story."

But it wasn't the end. Jo knew that. He'd carried that dismissal of his feelings around for years now. It was time for him to let it go and move forward with his life, whether it was with her or with someone else.

And the fact that this woman had insinuated that you couldn't have a friend and also be in love? That didn't make sense. A love without friendship would be very sad. She knew they could have both.

But if the kiss they'd just shared hadn't shown him that, what could? It had definitely taken them out of the friend zone as far as she was concerned.

"It's getting late. We better get back to the party," he said as he stood, reaching a hand down to her.

Placing her hand in his, she stood. It seemed as far as he was concerned things would just go back to normal. If only she could ignore the way their kiss had made her feel as easily as he was.

"So we just forget this ever happened? Maybe you can, but I don't know that I can do that."

He let go of her hand instantly. Withou
waiting for her, he started back up the beach
only speaking when she caught up with him
"Don't you see, Jo? What I feel for you i
too much to risk for some temporary fling
It would just end with hurt feelings becaus
there are too many emotions involved already
Do you really want that? The two of us angr
or hurt?"

She wanted to tell him that it didn't hav
to be that way. People had relationships tha
lasted forever. She'd been through hell in he
marriage, but she still believed there was ev
erlasting love. But even believing that, sh
couldn't promise him that what they ha
would last forever. He wouldn't believe he
if she did. He had compartmentalized rela
tionships into friendship or romantic fling
something that she knew now she coul
blame on his ex-fiancée.

He moved away from her, putting a cou
ple feet between them as they headed bacl
to the bar.

The rest of the walk was silent, except fo
when Moose decided to splash through th
waves at the edge of the shore. What mor
was there to say? One look at that stubbor

jaw of Casey's had told her he'd decided to put tonight behind them.

She hadn't realized just how far she'd gone when she'd left the bar. She'd only wanted to escape the humiliation of what she had done. Finally, the strings of lights that crisscrossed over the tiki bar's ceiling came into view. As they got closer, she was surprised that she couldn't hear the reggae music that usually blared across the outside speakers.

"Something must have happened," she said as they climbed the stairs to the bar that had been overflowing with people when she had left. Where had everyone gone?

"Hey, you guys." Jerry, the bartender for the night, came out of a small storage room that was the only enclosed part of the bar.

Unable to walk any farther, she took a stool at the bar. Her eyes went to the large television screen that was usually tuned to some sporting event for the crowd's entertainment. Tonight there was no rerun of a soccer or football game playing. Instead, it had been turned to a local news channel that was broadcasting a weather map showing the distinct outline of a hurricane.

"Where did everybody go?" Casey asked, taking a seat beside her at the bar.

"They all scattered about thirty minutes ago when the weather update came on. It seems Ileen has finally decided to make her move. Unfortunately, she's headed straight for us," Jerry said, before he went back into the storage area pulling a cart behind him.

Casey reached behind the bar and peeled the remote from its Velcro holder before turning up the volume so that they could hear what the local meteorologist was saying.

"Cuba is asking that its citizens evacuate inland as soon as possible as Hurricane Ileen, now a Category 3 hurricane, is expected to make landfall there before crossing back into the Atlantic, where we're now being told there is a strong probability that it will strengthen once again into a Category 3 hurricane as it heads toward the Gulf of Mexico. Monroe County Emergency Services has issued a mandatory evacuation of all nonresidents beginning at dawn this morning."

Jerry walked out of the storage room pulling a cart full of glass bottles behind him. It all made sense now. He was clearing out the bar's stockroom as fast as he could.

"Let me help," Casey said, taking the handle of the cart and following the man to where he had stacked up crates of alcoholic bottles and the clear glasses the bar used for serving.

"What do we do now?" Jo asked, after they had helped load the crates into Jerry's truck.

"I checked my phone. Alex hasn't called us in yet. We're both working tomorrow night so we'd better get some sleep while we can" Casey said as he dug his keys from his pockets.

Jo pulled her own keys out of her dress pocket and headed for her car with Moose beside her, glad that they had come in separate vehicles. She needed a few moments alone. Things between her and Casey had changed tonight and no matter if he wanted to or not, there was no going back. They both needed some time to figure things out.

As she loaded Moose into the car, she saw the box of dead roses Jeffrey had sent with his cryptic message. He might be planning to come after her, but she couldn't worry about her ex-husband now. Nor could she get sucked into the what-ifs that kept circling around in her head concerning her and Casey.

Because Casey was right. With Hurricane Ileen threatening the islands, this could be the last chance she got to sleep for a very long time.

# CHAPTER TEN

THEY'D JUST FINISHED their third flight going
back and forth to the mainland transporting
patients from the small Key West hospital
that were too sick to go by ground, when a
call came in for assistance at the request of
the coast guard medevac unit.

"Any idea what we're looking at?" Casey
asked the dispatcher as soon as they were in
the air. Familiar with the guys who were stationed at the local coast guard base, he was
more than a little surprised that they'd be asking for help from civilians.

"From the info we were given, it sounds
like a catamaran got caught in the waves
and turned over on its way back to land. It
was carrying twenty passengers. There are
two patients that need transport to Miami,
which is why they've called for help. They're
backed up with calls coming in from boats

from here to the Dry Tortugas. They're going to meet you on the beach and transfer the patients. That's all the information we have at this time. James has the coordinates for the pickup. If we hear anything else, we'll radio it to you. Be careful out there. The winds are starting to pick up off the coast. I wouldn't be surprised if you're not grounded in the next few hours."

"Thanks, for the info. Roger out," Casey said. The radio went off again, and he listened as James took instructions from the local Fire and Rescue for their landing spot.

"We're getting low on IV fluid supplies. We'll need to restock when we get back to headquarters," Jo said, stringing up a bag then setting it aside and starting on another one.

"Most of the patients from the hospital have been evacuated. Unless something else comes in, this might be our last flight," Casey said. As he went through the second bag of supplies, he could see that Jo was right. They were low on fluid and some of the meds used for sedation. Their last flight had been a motorcycle victim with a head injury who they'd been forced to intubate while in midflight.

He'd been a big guy, and it had taken a lot of meds to keep him under so that they could get him safely to a neurosurgeon at the nearest hospital. They had tried not to sedate him, but he'd become too combative to handle while ten thousand feet in the air.

"I hope so. I'm starting to drag," Jo said, the circles around her eyes telling him that she hadn't slept any better than he had.

"ETA five minutes," James called out to them.

Casey looked down at the road below him, still full of cars headed north out of town. They'd flown over Highway 1 several times that day, and the traffic remained bumper to bumper.

Two fire trucks came into view and Casey recognized the empty parking lot they would be landing in as part of Fort Zachary, but there was no sign of the coast guard medevac.

"I've got a visual," James relayed to the dispatch.

When the dispatch radioed back an all clear from the first responders on the ground, James began their landing.

"But where's our patients?" Jo asked as she studied the empty parking lot.

The skids hit the ground, and they each grabbed a bag and unloaded.

"Where's our patients?" Jo asked again, this time speaking to one of the firemen.

Before he could speak, Casey heard the slap of rotor blades overhead and the orange Dolphin came into view. Much bigger than the copter that Heli-Care used to transport patients, it was a multi-purpose, short-range recovery machine that could fly in all weather on its search and rescue missions.

"What you got for us?" Casey asked the two coast guardsmen as they began to unload the first patient.

"Two head injuries. This one is responsive. The other one isn't. Both were hypothermic, but we got them warmed up on the way in," one of the men yelled over the noise of the rotors.

"They've been married over forty years. They're here celebrating their anniversary," the other man said, joining them with the second patient and handing two ID cards to Jo.

"Why was there a tourist boat going out today?" she asked.

'Not today, last night. The owner thought he could get one more cruise in before the weather got bad," one of the guardsmen replied.

"You mean they were out there all night?" Jo asked, her voice reflecting her horror at the thought. "What about the rest of the passengers? And the crew?"

"We're bringing them in now. These two were the most critical. The rest are suffering from hypothermia and are banged up some, but they'll be okay. They managed to get back on the boat, but the mast was damaged. We'll be triaging them as we bring them in, but it looks like these are the only two that will need to be evacuated right now."

At that moment a strong wind picked up the sand and sent it flying in the air. Casey steadied the stretcher he helped push as the wind rocked it back and forth. Casey hoped the young man was right. The winds were picking up now, and before long it would be too late for anyone to fly. Even the coast guard had begun to evacuate its aircraft to other stations for safety. Only their all-weather Dolphin helicopters were staying behind to help with the evacuations and any rescue calls they received.

A voice came from the stretcher, and Casey

had to bend over to hear what his patient was saying.

"It was supposed to be romantic." The man's voice was weak, but Casey heard every word.

They loaded his patient first, and then Jo followed with her patient. They had the stretchers secured, and then they left the ground in record-breaking time.

The high winds were left behind the farther they got from the coastline. Heading north, away from the storm, Casey relaxed and got into the rhythm he and Jo always found when they worked together.

"Mr. Dugger." Casey read the name on the patient's ID, then stuck it in the top pocket of his flight suit. "How are you feeling? Any pain, nausea?"

"I'm okay. Just take care of Sandy. She went under. I couldn't find her." The man began to fight against the straps that restrained him.

"It's okay, Mr. Dugger. Sandy is right here beside you," Jo said. "We're going to get you both to the hospital."

Jo gave him a look then glanced pointedly at Casey's patient. Something was wrong with her patient, but she couldn't say anything in front of the woman's husband.

Casey looked over at Jo's monitor. The woman clearly had a change from the quick report they'd been given from the other crew, which had stated that both patients' vital signs were stable. Hypotensive, with tachycardia and a blood oxygen saturation in the eighties, the woman was about to crash if they didn't do something fast.

Without Jo asking, Casey pulled out a bag of norepinephrine and put it in her waiting hand. As Jo spiked the bag of IV medication, Casey checked his own patient's vital signs. Still stable. Good. It was going to take both of them to stabilize this man's wife.

"What's our ETA?" he asked James.

"Forty-five minutes," James said. "I got a call from Alex while you were loading up. We've been ordered back to the office after this flight."

"Got it," Casey said, not surprised that they were being called in. While he and Jo could go on working for hours, James had exceeded the flying time he was allowed per day. Besides, this was probably their last flight before the weather shut them down.

Casey looked back to Jo's monitor and was relieved to see that her patient's blood pressure had begun to turn around. The vasopressor was working, but her oxygen saturation was still low.

"King airway?" Casey asked as Jo opened their respiratory equipment box. She held up the laryngeal tube for him to see.

"What's going on? Is there something wrong with Sandy? Why hasn't she woken up yet?" Mr. Dugger asked, his voice getting weaker with every word until it became just a whisper. "I should have insisted we canceled the trip. But she was so excited. It was supposed to be romantic."

"I just need to ask you a few questions," Casey said, trying to get the man's attention from what was happening to his wife beside him, while he watched Jo carefully place the laryngeal tube. "Can you tell me the date?"

"I've got it," Jo said, attaching the tube to an Ambu bag, she began to squeeze the bag. When the woman's chest began to rise and fall in time with her ventilations, Casey bent over the woman and placed his stethoscope against her chest, listening for lung sounds.

"I've already told you. It's our anniversary," Casey's patient answered as Casey gave Jo a thumbs-up.

The woman's vital signs began to stabilize, and Casey continued to keep her husband occupied with his neuro assessment. The man had a laceration across his forehead, but appeared neurologically intact.

"ETA five minutes," James called over their headphones.

"Go ahead and call report," Casey said to Jo, then began another round of questions to his patient, hoping to keep the man from listening to Jo's report on his wife.

"Well, I don't want to do that again anytime soon," Jo said, twenty minutes later as they climbed back into the helicopter to head back to the island. "Can you imagine if we'd had to code the poor woman in front of her husband?"

"You both did great. That took real teamwork to do what you did and keep that man calm. I thought he was going to be a problem there for a minute," James said. "Not that I blame him. He had to feel helpless laying there beside her."

"Hopefully, his wife will recover and they

can come back someday for another anniversary," Casey said. He'd seen patients in worse condition survive.

"At least we gave her a chance by getting her here. With Highway 1 backed up with everyone evacuating, it would have taken hours to get them to the hospital," James said. "By the way, I don't understand why everyone was so surprised by you two getting involved, you know, romantically. Anyone can see you were meant to be together. My Mona told me months ago that she thought something was going on between you."

Casey knew that James's wife, Mona, considered herself a bit of a matchmaker, and she looked at him as a challenge. But James was right; he and Jo had always made a great team. She'd always been able to anticipate what he needed from her, and he'd been the same with her.

Memories of the night before filled his mind. Somehow their intuitiveness had led to the most passionate kiss of his life. It should have felt awkward, like kissing his sister. But there had been no awkwardness, no embarrassment. There'd only been a hunger for more. A hunger he'd gone to sleep with.

And a hunger that still ate at him. One he didn't know how to deal with. No matter how much he wanted her, she was still Jo. They'd promised to remain friends after this fake romance was over, and then they'd gone and complicated everything.

"What's the latest on the storm?" Jo asked. "Any changes?"

"It's almost stalled again, but it's track hasn't changed. They've officially put out tropical storm warnings for the Keys now. We're expecting hurricane warnings to come out soon," James said.

"Sounds like we better get home then and see what Alex has planned for us. There's still a lot of people on the island who are going to need help," Casey said as James took them up. It was better to concentrate now on the storm ahead instead of on what had changed between him and Jo. They'd have to talk about it eventually, but right then he'd rather ride out a hurricane than try to figure out what he was going to do about Jo.

# CHAPTER ELEVEN

"It's LIKE WATCHING your baby leave the nest," James said as the three of them watched the helicopter fly out of sight on its way to make one last transfer from the hospital to the mainland.

"Why didn't you fly out with them? I hear Heli-Care has rented rooms at one of the hotels to put up the staff that is evacuating," Jo said.

"Mona wouldn't leave without me. She's packed and waiting for me now. They say the bridges will be shut down by tonight. What about you two?" James asked.

It seemed Hurricane Ileen had finally decided that it was time to move, and Cuba was getting battered by the wind and rain the storm carried.

Jo looked over to where Casey stood. They'd been so busy that she hadn't really thought to make a plan. She had assumed that they would pack what they could and leave the island together. It's what they normally would have done. At least, it would have been before last night. It seemed the kiss on the beach that they'd shared had changed everything, though no one would know it by the way they had worked together for the last ten hours. They'd flown patient after patient out of the Keys as if that kiss had never happened. But it had. Eventually, when this storm had passed and things with Jeffrey were finished, they'd have to deal with it.

Her phone rang, and she pulled it from her pocket and saw that it was Casey's neighbor. They'd seen the woman that morning when they had left for work. Her son had been working at boarding up her windows before he and his mom evacuated, but that had been hours ago. "Hey, Ms. Terrie, what's up?"

"I'm so sorry, Jo. I just meant to leave that hammer we borrowed in case Casey needed it. I only left the door open for a moment, and then he was gone."

"Who was gone?" Jo asked, sure that her son would never have left his mother behind.

"It's Moose. He was there, and then he

wasn't. I didn't think he'd run off like that. But now my son says we have to leave and I can't find him anywhere," the woman said, her voice shaking with each word.

"Moose ran off?" Jo said. It didn't make sense. They'd left him safe inside the house, knowing they'd only be gone a few hours before flights got suspended.

There was a rustling on the phone and a man's voice came on. "Hey, Jo. Sorry about this. It's my fault, not Mom's. I went in to hurry her along and left the door open."

And Moose had seen a chance to make his escape. It wasn't the first time he'd set off on his own, but she'd always been there to catch him before he'd gone too far. And it'd always been around her apartment where everyone knew him.

"How long ago?" she asked as she tried to fight the panic that filled her. Moose was a big dog. Surely someone would have seen him and taken him in. His name and her phone number were on his collar.

"We've been looking all afternoon, and I'm afraid if we don't get on the road we'll never make it out of town."

She'd seen the bumper-to-bumper traffic

headed out of the Keys get longer and longer with each flight they'd flown. The man was right. "It's okay. Go ahead and leave. I'll head over there now."

Jo waited as the man apologized again and again before ending the call, then she headed for her car. She knew Casey would be right behind her. "Moose is missing. I'm going to start at the house and work outward. Can you call the shelter?"

The driver's side door opened as she unlocked the car and Casey got inside. "If he got picked up they should have called you, but I'll check with them. I'll check with the neighbors, too."

As he started on a string of phone calls, Jo searched her mind on where Moose could have gone. Her apartment was too far away, and she couldn't think of a reason he'd head back there. He'd settled in at Casey's house just fine. It was more likely he was just having a walk around town.

"Most everyone has already left town and the shelter isn't answering. I assume they're busy evacuating the animals," Casey said.

"I don't understand. He hasn't run off in

months, and then he stayed around the apartment complex," Jo said.

"He's probably right around the house somewhere. We'll find him, Jo."

Casey laid his hand across her thigh, and she had to stop herself from jumping. It was the first time he'd touched her since the night on the beach, and her body responded with a spark of delight that she immediately squashed. There would be no repeat of that night. Not until they had a chance to talk about what had happened. If they were going to make it out of this with their friendship intact, they'd have to face the fact that they were very much in lust with each other.

It only took fifteen minutes after they made it to Casey's house to rule out Moose being in the neighborhood. While Casey walked through the neighbor's backyards and called out for him, Jo drove slowly down the block, looking for anyone that she could ask if he'd been there. It wasn't like he was a poodle. Moose's size alone would make him stick out wherever he went.

"What if someone took him?" she said, when she stopped to pick Casey up at the end of the road. "You know how friendly he is. He could have just jumped inside someone's car and stuck his head out the window like he knew where he was going."

"No one picked him up," Casey said. "He has to be somewhere where there aren't a lot of people, otherwise someone would have checked his collar and called you. Where does he like to go?"

"They've closed all the shops downtown that give him treats. Besides that's too far away. There's the dog park, but that's probably locked up too. The only other place is the beach." That would make sense; it was one of Moose's favorite places in the world, but it was over three miles down the road.

"The closest one is Smather's Beach. Take a right on Flagler."

"Got it," Jo said as she pulled back onto the road. They'd only passed a handful of cars when they drove up to the beach parking lot. A few people dotted the sand, and there were some die-hard surfers who were enjoying the rough surf Hurricane Ileen was bringing in. "Should the surf be this rough already?"

"I don't know," Casey said as they walked up to the surf. "We've been so busy I didn't check to see if there have been any changes to the forecast."

"He could be anywhere," Jo said, looking up and down the beach and seeing no sign of her great, big, lovable dog. She'd had her doubts when Casey had talked her into taking Moose. It had been a challenge to keep him out of trouble in her small apartment, but they'd made it work. He was her best friend, besides Casey.

She had made lots of other friends on the island, but none of them could replace the big dog that had loved her the moment they met. She'd been beaten and broken by Jeffrey and had believed him when he'd said she was unlovable. She knew now that he was wrong. It had just been another way for him to abuse her. But she would never forget the love Moose had given her from the moment he'd come to live with her.

"We need to split up," she said to Casey.

"Let's see if anyone here has seen him first," Casey said.

They went from person to person with no one having seen a dog on the beach. She had finally convinced Casey that they would have to split up, when a surfer came out of the water and hurried toward them.

"Hey, are you the guys asking about the dog?" the young man, who couldn't have been more than nineteen, asked.

"Yes, have you seen him? He's a Great Dane, a really big Great Dane. He's black with white paws and he likes the water. He's usually splashing around in it." She knew she was rambling, but she couldn't seem to stop. "He ran away a few hours ago."

Casey put his arm around her, and she stopped talking. The guy was looking at her like she'd lost her mind, and she wasn't sure she hadn't. The last twenty-four hours had been draining, and she didn't think she could take much more.

"It sounds like the dog I saw. He was headed that way. I hope you find him," the teenager said before heading back into the surf.

"Thanks. Be careful out there. The surf is starting to look dangerous," Casey said.

She waved her thanks to all the young men and women sitting out on their boards, waiting for that next big wave. She had no way of knowing which of them had mentioned to the teenager that they were searching for her dog.

When Casey took her hand as she made her way through the deep sand, she knew it was only to help her keep up with him. It was something he had done before without either of them ever thinking about it. She shouldn't be thinking about it either. Not that way at least. Except it seemed her skin had become hypersensitive to even his lightest touch now. She couldn't ignore it. And it felt right. As if all the other times he'd touched her had only been a build up to what she felt now. A build up to last night and the kiss they'd shared. And if Casey knew she was thinking this way, he'd drop her hand like it was a hot poker.

She wasn't sure who saw whom first, her or Moose. He came at her like a bullet, knocking her down into the sand and licking her face like he hadn't seen her in months.

"He must have been scared he'd lost me," Jo said as Casey held the dog back while offering her a hand up. "It's okay, Moose."

"Are you okay?" Casey asked. "He doesn't usually jump people like that."

"But I'm not people. I'm his mom," Jo said.

"And I should be grounding him for the rest of his canine life."

As if knowing he was in trouble, Moose hung his head.

"It's okay, boy. We'll let it go this time," Casey said, patting the dog and hugging him. She'd known Casey was as worried as she was. He just wasn't going to let her know it.

"Let's just get home before this wind gets any worse," she said. The sun had already begun to set, and the wind had picked up since they'd arrived. The sand stung as the wind sent it splattering against her arms. She was glad she'd changed into jeans when she'd got off work instead of the shorts she usually wore.

When they made it back to the parking lot, they found it empty except for Jo's car. A note had been left under her windshield wiper advising her that Key West was under a mandatory evacuation order and they needed to leave the beach.

As they drove through town, the streets were abandoned, and almost all of the businesses and homes had been boarded up. "It's kind of creepy."

"Hopefully, it won't be like this for long,"

Casey said, though Jo could tell the deserted town bothered him too. The fewer cars they saw, the more worried she became. Something had changed in the last two hours while they had been hunting for Moose. The gusts of winds were getting stronger, and dark clouds had begun to roll in from the south.

"We might be in trouble. It looks like the timeline for Ileen's landfall has been moved up. They're predicting landfall in the early morning hours. The only good news is that it's moving now and hasn't had the chance to build its strength back up after landfall in Cuba. Still, they're predicting it to be a Category 2 before it reaches us. The hurricane hunters are set to fly out in the next two hours, but right now winds are measuring in the nineties. It's going to cause a lot of damage." Casey looked up from the app he was reading on his phone. "We've got eight hours before it hits."

Parking the car in the driveway, they both stared at Casey's little house. It had been built over seventy years ago and had been in Casey's family ever since. It wasn't a large house and the land, being in midtown, was more valuable than the house itself. But Jo knew it was the memories of Casey's grandmother that made him cherish the home.

"What do you want to do now?" she asked. If Casey wanted to stay in his home, she'd stay with him. But both of them knew that would not be safe. They could try to make it off the island, but the roads would still be packed and the bridges would be closed soon due to wind and flooding.

Her phone dinged, and she found she had missed four calls from Summer and had two text messages from Alex. "Alex says everyone has reported in except for the two of us. From the language he's using, he isn't very happy about that."

Casey's phone dinged and he read the message. "I got the same message. I'll text him back, though I don't know what to tell him. Staying here is an option, but not a good one. There are no shelters open on the island. All we can do is try to make it off."

He received another incoming message only seconds after he'd answered Alex. "He wants us at the hospital. He's volunteered to stay, and he says he's got a place for us."

"What about Moose? We can't take him into the hospital. Their administration will have a fit." She reached back and rubbed her big fur baby's head. "And I'm not going to leave him here."

"We'll sneak him in. I can guarantee the last thing administration will be worried about is having a dog in the building."

Casey looked around the small bare room. There were no pictures on the walls. No rugs on the vinyl floor. There wasn't even a chair to sit in. But tucked away inside a group of offices shared by the hospital's medical staff, the doctors' sleep room was the perfect place to hide Moose. With only one other physician remaining in the hospital besides Alex, and the two of them holding down the ER where a few patients had straggled in at the last moment, there wasn't any chance of the three of them being disturbed. There was just one problem with the setup. There was only one bed, and it was a small one at that. The only way they could share the bed would be with one of them almost piled atop the other one.

And that was either the worst idea or the best idea he'd had all day.

"We can take turns sleeping," he said. He didn't want to make Jo uncomfortable.

"What? You don't want to share this lovely bed with me? Don't worry, you're safe from me, tonight. I'm too tired right now to think about anything but sleep," Jo said, falling into the bed face-first. "Come on. You have to be as tired as I am."

He was tired. The last couple of days had been hard on them both. He should catch a few hours of sleep while he could. There would be a lot to do in the morning after the storm was gone. Only now, waiting for whatever Hurricane Ileen had planned for them, he was too wound up to rest. Then there was Jo. Climbing into bed with her was the worst thing he could do right now. Just the thought of lying beside her had him wanting more than just the kiss they'd shared the night before.

"I'm just going to check on Alex and see if there have been any updates on the weather station."

"Okay," Jo said, her voice muffled against the sheets, "chicken."

Chicken? Had she just called him a chicken?

He started to turn around. He'd show her he wasn't afraid of her or of climbing into that bed beside her. But the truth was, he was afraid. She should have been able to see how dangerous it would be to have the two of them piled into bed together. Instead, she was making a joke about it.

Being with Jo had always been relaxing; they could talk about anything. They could disagree on a subject without becoming angry with each other. His relationship with Jo was probably the least stressful one he'd ever had, which was especially surprising since she was female. It was one of the things that he liked most about being around her. And now all of that had changed because of one kiss on the beach. Wasn't that proof that mixing friendship with romance was a mistake?

When he shut the door behind him with a little too much force, he heard Jo laughing. At least one of them seemed to be having a good time.

Making his way down to the emergency room, he saw an ambulance bringing in a man on a stretcher.

"I can't believe you're still running calls," he said to one of the EMTs.

"It's our last. We've been told to stay here until the county emergency services clears us to go back out after the storm passes."

"I thought we were the only ones not smart enough to get off the island," Casey said, following them into a trauma room. By the way their patient's leg was twisted they didn't need an X-ray to know it was broken. "What did this guy do?"

"He was trying to board some windows in the dark when the wind blew his ladder over. He's lucky that he only broke a leg. It could have been his neck."

Casey moved on to the next room where he found Alex stitching up a man's hand that had been cut open by a homemade metal shutter. After all his offers of help were turned down, he made his way out to the ambulance bay. Sheets of rain were now slamming against the building, and in a few minutes he was soaked. This storm was coming in strong. No one else would be able to get to the hospital in this weather.

With nothing left to do, he went back up to where he had left Jo. Moose lifted his head and began to growl until he saw that it was Casey. Thankfully, Jo was sleeping soundly, so he grabbed the bag he'd packed and headed into the bathroom. His experience with storms throughout his childhood told him he better get a hot shower while he could. There was no telling when the county would be able to get the island's utilities back up. He'd spent two weeks without electricity once when a tropical storm had taken down the electrical lines on the island.

When he made it back to the bedroom, Jo had turned over on her side, leaving half the bed open. If he climbed in then and didn't move, it would be safe. He stretched out on the bed, careful not to wake her, and turned onto his side so he faced the opposite wall. It wasn't as nice as having his king-size bed to himself, but he'd slept in worse. All he had to do was stay on his side of the bed.

A hand on his leg woke him from the deepest sleep he'd had in weeks. "Casey, wake up. It's here."

What was here? "I don't know…" he started, then heard a crash outside that had him jumping up and covering Jo with his body.

He could hear the howling of the wind that seemed to circle the building. Alex had told him the hospital had been built to withstand even a Category 5 hurricane and they were in an interior room, so he knew they should be safe. Still, the sounds from outside left no doubt that this storm was destructive.

He felt Jo shiver against him. "It's okay, Jo. We're safe in here."

"I know that," she said, though her shivering didn't stop.

"This building is fairly new, and it's rated per the building code safe for the strongest hurricane possible. We're as safe as we could be anywhere on the island," he said, wrapping his arms around her. "I won't let anything happen to you."

"I know that," she said again. "I'm not scared of the storm."

He eased back and tried to make out her features in the dark. "Then what's wrong? Are you cold?"

"Cold is the last thing I am right now," she said as one of her hands slid up his bare abdomen to his chest.

His breath caught and his heart did a skip and then a jump. "We probably should see if Alex needs any help downstairs."

"I'm not getting on the elevators. If the generators go out we could get stuck there. And the stairs have all those windows. I'm afraid you're stuck here with me right now. Just listen to that wind. Isn't it amazing?"

He took a breath and relaxed as best he could while still keeping Jo protected. The wind continued to blow outside, its loud moan seeming to travel around the top of the building. The power of it was humbling. There was nothing fiercer than Mother Nature. Never had he been reminded of that as much as he was at that moment.

"How long do you think this will go on?" Jo asked, snuggling deeper into his arms.

She knew what she was doing to him. There was no way she could miss the evidence that holding her like this had aroused him. He was hard, and his body was anticipating something that he knew should not happen. "I don't know. It's a good size storm. If we're directly in its path, it will all stop when the eye passes over. But it won't be for long. Then it will all start again."

"Is it terrible that even though I know it's plowing through the island damaging homes and businesses and possibly causing deaths, that I still find the force of it thrilling? The power of it reminds me of just how small and insignificant we all are. Up here, tonight, it's as if we are all alone in the world."

He knew that feeling of aloneness. He'd been filled with it a lot lately, that was until Jo had moved in. He'd forgotten how much he'd dreaded going home after a long shift to his empty home.

Her bare legs rubbed against his, and he realized as her damp hair tickled his nose that he hadn't been the only one to take advantage of the shower. Now only his shorts and her oversize T-shirt seemed to separate them. When her hand slipped down his chest to his abdomen, then further, he gasped.

"What if we never get a chance to be together like this again? All alone in this room, no one to interrupt us. Just you and me and this one night together. Would it be so bad if for just one night you let down those walls and see where whatever this thing is between the two of us takes us?" Jo asked, her hand stilling on the button of his shorts. "Aren't you tempted to find out?"

"We're going to be okay, Jo. This won't be our last night," Casey said as he shook his head, trying to shake away the fog of desire that had spiraled around him with her words.

Was he tempted? Oh, yes. But still, he knew the morning would come, and with it reality.

"Are we?" she asked, one hand coming up to his cheek, soft and cool against his overheated skin.

The darkness of the room kept him from seeing her expression, but he understood what she meant. It wasn't the hurricane she was afraid of. With that kiss they'd shared, they'd broken their own rule, shattered it with the passion that burned between them that night on the beach. He'd tried to convince her to put it behind them. It would be easier for them to go back to their normal lives that way.

It might be too late to fix what they'd broken. How could they when his body continued to respond to hers this way? Could they go back to being only friends now? He didn't know.

But would one night together change that? The line had already been crossed. Maybe this was the only way to put it behind them. Maybe they could end this overwhelming need to finish what they had started on the beach by letting it burn its way out.

Something outside crashed against the building and he held her closer. Her mouth was so close, her breath warm against his lips, he had no strength against this. His lips moved over hers, for comfort or pleasure, he didn't know. Then her mouth opened under his and the heat of it made him forgot every reason he'd ever had that this wasn't a good idea.

He took his time, stretching the kiss out until they both needed to come up for air. His lips traveled down her neck, and her moan echoed the sounds of the wind. Her tongue, warm and soft against his ear, had pleasure shooting down through the length of his shaft.

Clothes were peeled off, one by one, each revealing a treasure for him to explore. Inside he knew that this was his friend, Jo, but here, lying with her naked in his arms, she was his lover tonight.

As the wind raged outside, he buried himself inside of her. Her heat surrounded him, drawing him deeper until there was no him or her. They were one.

Her legs wrapped around him and they rode out the storm together. He lost track of time. He forgot about all the ways this could complicate his life. Jo. The taste of her, the smoothness of her skin, the way her hands and mouth moved against him; she was his whole world tonight. Something broke inside of him as her body shuddered in his arms, flooding him with an emotion he couldn't name. Happiness? Pleasure? No. This was something more. And it scared him.

"I love you Casey Johnson," Jo whispered in his ear.

His eyes shut tight, even as his body trembled with pleasure. So many women had said those words after they'd shared their bodies with him. They meant nothing. Not to him. Anna had whispered the same words the first time they'd made love. He'd believed her then.

And this was Jo. His best friend Jo. After what she'd been through with her ex, she was vulnerable. It was understandable that she could be emotional right now. That was all it was. Tomorrow, when the storm had passed and the sun came out, she'd want to take back those words.

As the storm still raged, he held Jo until her breathing became slow and deep. He was so confused by emotions that didn't make sense to him. But the night would be over soon and they'd have to face the damage that had been done. They'd rebuild what was needed, and the island would come back even stronger. He just hoped he and Jo could do the same.

# CHAPTER TWELVE

Jo woke up in a tangle of legs and arms. She lay still, enjoying the weight of Casey's body on hers, and she listened to…nothing. There was no howling wind or slashing rain. There were no noises coming from the rooms around them. No people. No storm. Everything was quiet. It was like she and Casey were the only two people left in the world. It had been the same last night when they'd made love. With the storm outside, she'd felt totally alone, except for Casey. She'd felt safe and cared for in his arms. She'd felt…loved.

So she'd opened her mouth and let her sex-boggled brain convince her to say the last words Casey wanted to hear from her. She'd managed to keep them bottled up inside of her for so long, why now? Maybe that was the reason. Because she'd known if she didn't say them then, while Casey held her, that she might never get the chance?

And what was so wrong with telling someone you loved them? Wasn't that what everyone wanted? To be loved. Well, everyone but Casey if he was to be believed. The man had let an old heartbreak destroy his ability to understand that feeling love wasn't a weakness, it was a gift. Until he figured that out there would be no hope for anything more than friendship with him, and she knew now that would never be enough for her.

And now she had to look at him and hope she hadn't made a complete fool of herself. The eerie quietness of the room penetrated through her thoughts. It really did seem that they were the only people in this building. That thought sent a shiver down her. She'd seen too many apocalyptic movies that had ended this way.

"Casey, wake up. We've got to get downstairs," Jo said, untangling her legs with his until she could stand, then almost tripping on Moose where he lay beside the bed.

"What's wrong?" Casey asked, raising his head.

"We need to check on the others." She

reached for the light switch, and some of her panic eased when light flooded the room. "We have power. Maybe the storm wasn't that bad."

"It might be the backup generators. They kick in when the power goes off. Alex said the hospital can run on those for three days. The power company should have power back to the hospital by then." The messy, flop of his blond curls hanging over his green eyes and the sight of his bare, sculpted chest made her want to climb back into the bed beside him. If only she could. But from the hooded look he was giving her, she knew he was already working to bring up those walls between them.

Grabbing her bag from the floor, she went into the bathroom and dressed. When she returned, she found Casey dressed and waiting for her. When he didn't make eye contact, she knew things between them were still on shaky ground.

Why had she opened her mouth? She'd ruined everything. They'd had sex. Couldn't she just accept that was all it had been?

She looked away from him. Right now wasn't the time to talk about it. The storm was gone and now they needed to make sure everyone downstairs was safe.

"Moose, stay," she said as she filled one of his bowls with the water from the water bottle she'd packed, then filled the other bowl with his dog food.

"We'll be right back," Casey said, patting the dog. "You were a very brave boy last night, and I'll take you outside as soon as I know it's safe."

Moose looked at him with trusting eyes and then started on his food.

"Thank goodness he isn't afraid of storms. There's no way the staff wouldn't have heard him even with the floors between us if he'd started howling, though they probably would have thought it was just the storm," she said, waiting for Casey to say something, anything, to break the tension in the room.

When he only nodded, she gave up. Knowing Casey, it was possible he'd never say anything about last night again. He was good at ignoring anything that made him uncomfortable.

Part of her hoped he would pretend nothing had happened while part of her wanted to have it out in the open. Just get it over with and see what happened.

Why? Because she thought last night had meant as much to him as it had to her? If it had, there was no sign of it this morning. He was making it plain that he was uncomfortable with her now. That wasn't something a man who had spent the night discovering that they had more than just a friend relationship would do.

They took the stairs, stopping at every floor to look out the windows that opened to the back of the building. There were trees down and a dumpster mysteriously in the middle of the parking lot, but that was all the damage she could see. She looked for her car and was relieved to see that it had escaped being squashed by the fallen trees. Not all of the staff had been so lucky. She knew Casey had to be anxious to check on his home too, but first they needed to check in with Alex.

Stepping into the ER, she found it almost deserted. The unit coordinator sat at her desk and there were a couple rooms occupied by patients, but the rest of the staff was missing.

"Where is everyone?" Casey asked when they passed one of the nurses.

"They've just stepped outside to look around," he said, before continuing to one of the patients' rooms.

They stepped out into the ambulance bay to find Alex along with some of the nurses looking up at the sky. Jo had been so busy looking at the ground on the way down the back stairs that she had never looked up.

The sky was blue and cloudless, and the sun seemed to shine brighter than she had ever seen it. It was hard to believe that there had been a storm just a few hours ago. It was as if the hurricane had washed the sky clean and left it vibrant and sparkling when it had moved on.

They heard the wail of a siren and turned as an ambulance pulled into the bay. "It looks like it's time to get back to work," Alex said.

"If you don't need us here, we can head over and check out HQ," Casey offered.

"My relief should be here in a few hours, and I'm headed home to see what damage I've got at the house. I want to get Summer and the babies home as soon as it's safe," Alex said. "Check out your own place on the way to Heli-Care. We can station here at the hospital if we need to if we get the helipad cleared.

I know I'll be getting calls from the corporate office soon."

"I'll text you some pictures as soon as we get there," Jo said, already following Casey inside.

"Don't do anything stupid. There will be power lines down all across the island, and a lot of the roads will still be flooded. Take the interior roads," Alex said, before heading into a trauma room where the EMTs were unpacking their patient.

"Those guys are going to be busy today," Casey said as they left the ER and headed back upstairs for Moose.

The trip to Casey's place should have only taken fifteen minutes. Instead, they spent over an hour weaving their way through street after street that had been blocked with fallen trees or flooding. They ran into an officer who advised them on areas to avoid after he checked their IDs to make sure they were residents who belonged on the island.

When they finally made it, they were relieved to see that except for some shingles that had been stripped from the roof, Casey's house remained undamaged. Ms. Terrie's house hadn't been so lucky.

"She's going to be so upset when she sees this," Jo said as they looked at the tree that had crashed through the top of the woman's home.

"I'll come back and put a tarp over it for now," Casey said, shaking his head. "It's not much though. She'll need a new roof, and there will be water damage from the rain that she'll have to deal with."

"We'll help her, just like we helped Lucy," she said. It would take months to repair the damage to the island, but everyone would pitch in to help. That's what people did here.

They left Moose safe inside the house and changed Jo's car for Casey's truck, which would be safer on the flooded roads.

"I wonder how long it will take till things get back to normal," Jo asked. "That officer said that they were already sending engineers out from the county to check the bridges."

"If the bridges are okay, they'll start letting residents in today," Casey said.

"Good. It's weird being here without everyone. I don't like it."

"You don't like being alone with me?" he asked. Jo searched his face, looking for any sign that he was serious. Any sign that he wanted to talk about the night they'd just shared. The smile disappeared from his face. Yeah, he was thinking about the night they had just spent alone.

They had to face it. They couldn't keep pretending like nothing had happened between them. Even if he considered it just a one-night fling, she knew it was more.

Those three little words she'd spoken had changed everything. She could make an excuse for it. She was overwhelmed by the storm, by the passion. Casey would accept any excuse she gave just to get out of having to face it. Wouldn't that be the best thing to do? Just let him think she was just being "emotional" as he called it?

They'd crossed several lines, broken all the rules, and now she had to accept more than half the responsibility.

She'd been the one who'd reached out for him last night. Yes, part of it had been the storm. Lying in the bed all alone, not knowing what was happening outside of that little hospital room had been scary. She'd wanted him to hold her.

Telling Casey that was the reason she had declared her love for him would only be partly lying. A part of her had been affected by the storm and by their lovemaking. Would it really be that bad to take the cowardly way out and pretend that was all it had been?

If only she hadn't felt the truth in those words. She loved Casey. She couldn't deny it any longer. Why should she? Because she was scared? Maybe once that would have been true, but not now. She'd been through too much to let something like fear keep her from admitting her feelings for someone. She wasn't the woman she'd been when she'd married Jeffrey. She stood up for herself now, and she went after what she wanted.

*And if Casey can't give you what you want? What will you do then?*

"I don't know what to say," she said, refusing to let fear keep her from doing what she knew she needed to do. But how did you tell someone that you loved them when you knew it was the last thing they wanted to hear?

"What do you mean?" Casey said, his eyes never leaving the road ahead of them.

"We need to talk about it, Casey. You know that."

"Why?" he asked. "What's there to say? It happened. It's over."

"What's over? Us?" Her voice was not much more than a whisper. How could he be so cold? How could he dismiss what they had shared? Or was that fear she heard in his voice? She should know. She'd let fear of rejection keep her from admitting her feelings for Casey for years.

He stopped the truck in the middle of the road and turned toward her. "Look, we got caught up pretending to be involved. I should have known this could happen. We let down our guard for a few minutes. We won't do it again."

"What do you mean 'we'?" she asked, her voice rising.

"We're a team. That's what we do," he said, his own voice rising now.

"A team? So what, last night was just teamwork?" How could he be so smart yet so dense? How could he not see what they could have together?

"It was a mistake. The storm and the situation was overwhelming. We got caught up in everything around us. It happens," he said.

"It doesn't happen to me," she said, refusing to take the easy way out of this. Didn't he know she could be as stubborn as he was?

He started the truck and headed back down the road as if the subject was closed. Well, it wasn't closed as far as she was concerned. "We can't pretend it never happened just because it makes you uncomfortable. It did happen. We made love and I told you that I love you."

She watched, waiting for his next move. His hands tightened on the wheel until his fingers went white, but he didn't respond to her words. Had she pushed too hard?

Her phone rang, startling her. For a few minutes she'd forgotten the world outside of the two of them. "Hey, Alex. We're almost at headquarters."

She listened as her boss relayed a call for help from the local emergency services. While a part of her asked the appropriate questions, another part of her withdrew inside of herself. She'd been here before when she'd realized that Jeffrey didn't really love her. He'd only wanted her as a submissive wife who would represent him in the perfect world he thought he could create. Casey didn't want her love either. He only wanted her friendship. He wanted his life free of all the messy emotions that made up a real life.

"Emergency services received a call for help off of North Roosevelt, but they only have the one crew up and running and they're tied up. Apparently the caller was frantic. Alex asked if we could respond."

"Address?" Casey asked as he made a U-turn in the middle of the road, the action fast and sharp, sending her into the passenger door. She grabbed the handle above the door as the truck swerved back onto the road.

"They didn't have an address. The caller said he'd be on the road to meet us." Jo braced herself as Casey hit the gas pedal. What was wrong with him? Casey never drove this way. He was always in control when he was behind the wheel. "Slow down. If you wreck us, there'll be no one to help these people."

She relaxed her hold on the door handle as their speed slowed, but she didn't let go. She was headed into uncharted territory. She didn't know what to expect when they reached the person who had called for help. She didn't know what to expect from Casey now that she had been honest about her feelings. All she could do was hold on for the ride.

# CHAPTER THIRTEEN

CASEY TRIED TO loosen his hold on the steering wheel. Jo's insistence that they discuss the night before while he was still trying to come to terms with it was too much right now. Hearing her declaration of love had rocked something inside of him. He was suddenly filled with emotions that he didn't know how to handle. Fear, for what he and Jo could lose, along with a surprising hope that maybe there was something more between them. What if what he felt for Jo was more than friendship? Or were the two of them just confused by this unexpected passion between them? And what if it was love? That brought about a whole new level of fear. He'd almost destroyed his life after his and Anna's breakup. How much worse would it be if things between him and Jo went wrong?

His whole life felt out of control, and losing

control was not something he did. If you lost control, you made mistakes. He couldn't afford to make mistakes. Not when someone's life might be depending on him.

"All I have in the truck is a first-aid kit," he said, trying to get their attention on the job ahead of them. "You would think they would have gotten more information from the caller."

"Alex said they lost their connection to the caller, and he didn't answer when they called back. Fire and Rescue said they would be there as soon as possible," Jo said.

They backtracked to First Street then took it to North Roosevelt. He had grown up on this island and knew every road and pothole. If you gave him an address, he could find it. Without an address all they could do was keep their eyes open and hope they found the 911 caller before it was too late.

"Where do we go from here?" Jo asked.

Wasn't that the question of the day? He had no idea where they were going. And to think a couple weeks ago he had total control of his life.

"You decide. Left or right?" he asked her.

Their argument had left him drained and feeling that whatever he said would be wrong.

"Go right and you never go wrong, right?" she said.

"Sure," he replied, unable to put any enthusiasm into his voice. They'd only made it a couple blocks before they came to a spot where the road had been washed away, leaving an opening that even his truck couldn't drive over.

"What do we do now?" Jo asked.

"I guess we walk," he said, opening the door and climbing out. "I'll get the first-aid kit."

"We don't even know if we are going the right way," Jo said as they made their way down and over the sand and water that was left where there used to be a road.

"There's something big there on the right side of the road. Let's check that out. If we can't see anything from there, we'll turn around." Casey wasn't sure what he was seeing. A bus? Someone's shed? It could be anything that the storm had picked up and dumped on the side of the road.

As they got closer, he started to make out

the squared off sides of a large vehicle. "It's an RV that's been flipped."

They were only twenty yards away when he saw the man sitting on the side of the road, a small dog at his side. "Hey, did you call for help?" Jo called as she hurried over to him.

"Oh, thank God you're here," the man said as he tried to stand.

"Don't move," Casey said, getting to the man's side and easing him back down onto the road. "Where are you hurt?"

"Me? I'm okay. It's my wife. She's in there. I can't get her out," the man said, his breathing fast and ragged. "She's pinned down. I just managed to get out myself a few minutes ago. I had to leave her."

Casey looked at the RV lying on its side. The thing was as big as a bus. "What happened?" he asked the man.

"We left too late. We thought we had time. We didn't want to leave the RV behind, so we packed it up for the trip," the man said. His color was good, but he was still out of breath.

"Casey, I think I can get in," Jo said, calling from the other side of the vehicle.

"I'll be right back," Casey said to the man then rushed to where Jo was climbing up on what would have been the RV's top. "What are you doing?"

"If I can get to the top, there should be a window I can get in through," she said as she climbed higher.

"Get down and I'll do it," he said as she reached the top. His heart pounded and he started up behind her. "We're not Fire and Rescue. We're not trained for this."

"I'm just going to look inside. If I can't get in, I'll climb down."

He glanced around them for something he could use to describe their location and situation then texted the information, knowing his boss would find a way to get them some help. He waited till he got a thumbs-up from Alex, then he headed up after Jo.

He caught up to her as she pulled herself onto the top of the vehicle. "Be careful up there."

"I'm okay. This thing is huge. It's not going anywhere," Jo said as she knelt and looked over the side at him.

"That's what they thought last night." All the blood in his body rushed to his feet when she let go of the side and stood up. "What are you doing? Just wait a moment till I get up there."

"I'm just going to look into the window. I'll be right back."

He looked for something he could use to pull himself over the side of the vehicle. How had she gotten up there?

"I can see her," Jo called from where she had disappeared on the top.

"Ma'am, can you hear me?" she called as she knocked against what he assumed was a window. "Casey, she's not responding. There's a cabinet on top of her. I think it's a pantry because there's cans of food everywhere. If I had a way to get this window open, I could drop down beside her."

"The windows are probably locked. Is there a door?" Casey asked as he finally made his way over the top. He knelt, making sure he could keep his balance, before standing and making his way over to her.

Looking in the window Jo was leaning over, he could see the woman where she lay flat on her back. "Something has to be on top of that cabinet or they would have been able to push it off. The whole inside of this thing is destroyed. It's amazing that it didn't break in two."

He stood and headed to the front of the vehicle. "This has to be how her husband got out."

Casey tried to pull the door open but it was stuck. He looked around for something to pry it open. Where was Fire and Rescue? "If he got out this way, it must have locked when it shut."

"There's a window open here," Jo called from behind him.

Giving up on the door, he joined her where one of the small windows had been slid open. There was no way he was fitting through that. "We should have help here soon. They'll have the equipment to get the door open."

"I think I can get through," Jo said as she moved over the window and placed her feet into the opening.

"And do what? You can't get her out of there. We should wait until Fire and Rescue arrive. I texted Alex our location before I climbed up here. He'll get us some help."

"She's been down there for hours. I can at least assess the situation and let you know what we're going to need so you can forward the information to Alex."

"It's too dangerous. You could fall on something getting down there. We should wait here for help." Couldn't she see the danger? If she fell and broke something, he'd have two patients.

"Let me do this. It's not that far down. You can lower me most of the way."

She climbed into the small opening and he grabbed her hand, lowering her inside as far as he could, stretching his arm down inside the RV.

"Let me go. There's an overturned chair here. I can make it from this point," Jo said as she let go of his hand.

He hesitated then pried his fingers from her hand. He saw the top of her head as she dropped to the bottom with a thud. "Are you okay?"

"I'm fine. I'm going to head to the back," Jo said before disappearing from his view.

As he headed to the back, he heard a siren in the distance. It sounded like they were coming in from the north so they would be able to avoid the washed-out road.

He needed to go check on the woman's husband, but he couldn't leave Jo even though there was nothing he could do to help her from where he was.

"I think she has a fractured hip. We'll need to stabilize it when we take her out of here. Her pulse is fast and weak. She's awake but not oriented. There's a laceration to the back of her head. She'll need a CT when she gets to the ER. There also appears to be an open fracture of the femur. It's hard to see because of the cabinet on top of her. She's going to need an ortho surgeon. Do you to have a C-collar in your first-aid kit? I need to stabilize her neck. I wouldn't rule out a cervical fracture from the way she's laying. I don't know how her husband got out of here. The whole place is a danger zone."

"I've got one. I'll go down and get it and some bandages for her head too. Don't move while I'm gone."

He made the trip down the side of the RV to where he'd left his first-aid kit and back up as quickly as possible. The siren he'd heard earlier didn't sound any closer. They must have run into some debris on the road or another place where the road had been washed out.

"What are you doing?" he hollered after sticking his head through the open window and seeing Jo trying to lift the cabinet from the woman.

"I wanted to try to prop this cabinet up so I could get to her leg, but it won't budge."

"I'm going to try to get the collar as close to you as possible," he said, easing his head out of the window so that he could place his hand holding the collar inside. He threw the plastic-wrapped foam collar as far as it would go, then pulled his arm out and stuck his head in to see where it had gone.

"I've got it," Jo called as she scrambled up the side of an overturned couch to retrieve it.

He watched as she made it back to the woman and carefully placed the collar while explaining to her injured patient what she was doing. It wasn't much, but maybe it would protect the woman if she began to move around.

"Okay. Throw me the bandages," Jo said as she headed back toward the open window.

He saw the look of surprise on her face before he realized she had slipped on something on the floor. As if in slow motion, he watched as her body was pitched forward and came down, her head slamming onto what looked like the edge of a cabinet.

"Jo?" he called through the window, expecting her to lift her head and reassure him that she was fine. But instead she lay as still as death. Death? No. Not Jo.

"Jo, answer me. Are you okay?" His voice carried through the RV, loud and booming. But she didn't answer.

He rushed over to the door he'd tried earlier and tried again to pull it open. It didn't budge. The door seemed to be the only thing on the vehicle that hadn't been broken. He looked inside its glass opening and saw that the handle appeared to be locked as they had assumed earlier. Taking his T-shirt off, he wrapped it around his fist and began punching through the glass. After a few good punches, the glass began to shatter. Another punch, and he had a hole big enough to get his hand in so that he could remove the rest of the glass. In seconds, he had the glass removed and he reached in and over to the handle, lifting it carefully while holding the outside door handle.

Swinging the door open, he lowered himself onto the edge of the driver's seat then made his way back to where Jo lay. She moaned when he reached her, and he took a deep breath. Okay. She was injured, but alive.

"Stay still," he told her. He moved a pillow and basket that lay between them and carefully examined the laceration across her forehead. "Jo, can you open your eyes for me?"

"Fire and Rescue," a voice announced as a tall man came through the door, which had been left open. He was followed by a young woman Casey recognized. "You're Casey from Heli-Care, right? They said we were to meet you. Is this our patient?"

"I thought you'd never get here. No. Your patient is over there. She has an open femur fracture and a laceration to the back of her head. Possible hip fracture too. Jo put a C-collar on her neck," Casey said.

"Is that Jo?" The young woman moved down beside him as her partner made his way to the other woman. "What happened?"

"She fell. Hit her head on this counter—" Casey pointed to the stone counter behind him "—and lost consciousness. It just happened, but she's not coming around like she should."

"We had to stop and move some downed trees on the way in. The roads are a nightmare right now, but there's an ambulance behind us that can transport both of them."

Jo moaned again, but her eyes still didn't open. The relief he'd felt when he'd realized she was alive was starting to drain away. If it was just a concussion, she should be waking up by now. If it was something more serious, like a brain bleed, she needed to get to the hospital as soon as possible.

An EMT dropped down into the RV and looked around the scene. "This is a mess. Where's the patient? Wait, is that Jo?"

As Casey explained once more how Jo had been injured without taking his eyes off her, dread began to fill him. Why wasn't she waking up?

"Okay," the EMT said, "we need to get both of these women out of here fast. Jo's going to be the easiest to get out, so we take her first. My partner and one of the Fire and Rescue guys is bringing up a basket so we can strap them in and lower them down the side. Casey, once we get Jo out, we're going to need you to help us lift that cabinet off our other patient."

He started to protest, but stopped. The faster

they got the other woman out, the faster they could get both of them to the hospital.

The EMT was right. They'd managed to get Jo out of the RV quickly and down in the metal basket to a second EMT waiting below, but getting the other woman out from under the debris while stabilizing her hip and fractured leg had proven to be a challenge. As soon as they had her lowered safely down, Casey climbed off the RV to check on Jo. When he saw that she was still unconscious, he almost panicked.

As they started to close the ambulance doors, she moaned again, but her eyes fluttered open this time. A confused look crossed her face, and then her eyes shut again. "Casey?"

"I'm here," he said as he grabbed one of the doors.

"We've got to go. He'll see you at the hospital," the EMT said as he shut the door in Casey's face.

As the ambulance pulled away, Casey looked over to where the Fire and Rescue crew was talking to the older man. He'd forgotten about the woman's husband. He had to be as worried about his wife as Casey was about Jo.

"How about I give you a ride to the hospital?" Casey asked. "They can get you checked out while you're waiting to see your wife."

"This is all my fault. She wanted us to leave yesterday, but I wouldn't listen," the man said. "I thought we had time. Last night, when the storm came in and everything was rocking back and forth in the RV, I didn't know if we would survive the night. I sat there helpless beside her, unable to get her free. All I could think about was what my life would be like if I lost her. I have nothing without her. I am nothing without her. We're two halves that make up this one whole."

Casey couldn't imagine what this man had gone through during the night. While he'd held Jo in his arms as the storm had passed, this man had lived through a nightmare.

"The doctors at the hospital will take good care of her."

"They won't let me bring Sugar with me, and I can't leave her here alone. Paula would have my head." The man petted the small, wiry-haired dog of undeterminable breed. The dog hadn't made a sound since they'd arrived, and Casey wondered if it was in some kind of shock too. "My name's Jack."

"I'm Casey and I think they'll make an exception. If not, I'll find someone to watch her." Casey helped the man up. He watched as Jack settled on his feet then headed toward Casey's truck.

"They said your girlfriend was hurt helping to care for Paula. I'm sorry for that," Jack said as soon as he climbed in the truck.

"Her name is Jo. She's my friend. My best friend," Casey said, though why he felt the need to correct the man he didn't know.

"That's the best kind of girlfriend, don't you think?" Jack said as he petted the dog in his lap. "Of course it doesn't always work out that way. Sometimes there's a spark of chemistry that sets things going between two people. Then they have to learn to be friends or it doesn't work out."

"Is that what happened with you and your wife?" Casey asked. He wanted to hit the gas and race to the hospital, but he knew he couldn't do that with Jack in the truck.

"We've known each other most of our lives. We didn't always like each other, but that changed when we made it to high school. I enlisted in the navy as soon as I graduated, and we were married after I graduated from boot camp. Moved all over the country while in the service. We raised four kids, and now have seven grandkids. There's another on the way. Paula always said she wanted ten grandkids, and she might get them."

Casey thought of the condition the woman had been in when she'd been loaded onto the ambulance. He hoped she would be around to see those ten grandkids.

They pulled into the hospital parking lot, and Casey stopped to let Jack and his dog out at the front door. After promising to come back to take the man to the emergency room, he parked the truck.

When they entered the emergency room, one of the nurses spotted the dog and opened her mouth to object, then saw Casey shake his head and she quickly looked away. He led Jack over to a trauma room where he could see the doctor examining his wife before he went in search of Jo.

"She's in CT, Casey," the unit coordinator said when he approached her desk. "They'll bring her back to trauma room two when they're finished."

"Can you let me know when the CT results come back?" he asked. He'd imagined all kinds of complications Jo could have from the trauma to her head.

"We don't have an in-house radiologist due to the storm, but we're sending them off to a radiologist in Miami to be read. It will take a little longer. I'll let Dr. Patel know you're here, though. He's busy working on the other patient the EMTs brought in. I sure wish we could get Heli-Care in here."

"I thought Alex was working on that," he said, at the same time remembering that he and Jo had never made it to check out what damage had been done to their headquarters. "He'd said we might be able to fly in here."

"Our maintenance man has been trying to clear the helipad all morning. It's just too much for one person, and we're short-staffed. There's no one to send to help him."

"Let me make some phone calls," Casey said. He walked by the trauma room where he'd left Jack and saw the man clutching his wife's hand as he held the little dog in his other arm. From the look on Jack's face, the news he had received from the doctor wasn't good. The woman needed care that couldn't be provided here. And Jo? If she had a serious head injury and needed surgery, there was no one here who could do it.

He hit the callback button on his phone as he made his way out of the ambulance bay. If Alex could get a helicopter here, he would find a place for it to land.

# CHAPTER FOURTEEN

BY THE TIME Casey and the maintenance man had cleared the helipad, the sound of rotor blades could be heard in the sky. The local ER doctor had made arrangements for both Jack's wife and Jo to be transferred to a receiving hospital in Miami while Casey had got ahold of Roy and Alex to get a flight arranged. Roy had been the first pilot they could contact, and Dylan had volunteered to help Casey with the two patients.

"I don't think this is necessary," Jo protested as she was loaded on the helicopter. "I just have a headache. You need to concentrate on taking care of the woman from the RV. She's the critical one."

"You have a subdural hematoma from hitting your head. The neurosurgeon Dr. Patel spoke with wanted you flown into Miami so you can be watched closely in ICU in case it expands and you need surgery." Casey reminded her of what the doctor had explained just minutes before the helicopter had arrived.

"I heard the doctor," Jo grumbled.

"Nurses do make the worst patients," Dylan said from beside him. "I'll take care of Jo, and we can still tag team the trauma patient."

Casey had spoken to Jack before loading his wife and assured him he'd call as soon as possible. Jack planned to take the first flight to Miami as soon as the airport was opened back up.

Once Paula had been loaded and secured, Casey was busy handling the number of IV drips that were required to keep the woman sedated and comfortable. Since Paula would be taken directly to surgery from the ER—after the flight—Dr. Patel had chosen to intubate her before their flight.

It only seemed like minutes before the shoreline of Miami came into view. Looking over at Jo, he was glad to see that her color was good and her respiration even. Her vital signs registering on the monitor were stable too. "No neuro changes?"

"No changes. She's stable right now," Dylan said. They both knew that with a head-bleed things could change quickly. "She had to have taken a pretty hard knock to her head to get that bleed."

Just thinking about the moment when Jo had fallen made his stomach churn. He was a seasoned nurse in a job where he saw the worst of the worst injuries, but seeing Jo lying there, not moving. Nothing had ever affected him that way before. It was like his own life had stopped in that instant.

Looking at her now, her eyes closed and her chest moving in rhythmic motions, gave him a peace of mind that he hadn't had since that moment. She was going to be okay. She had to be.

He looked back over at his own patient and thought about Jack. He'd felt so bad leaving the man behind. He knew he wouldn't want to be the one watching that helicopter fly away with Jo while he was left on the ground.

"ETA five minutes," Roy called over their headphones.

"I'll call report on both of them, if that's okay with you," Casey volunteered, then radioed into the hospital frequency when Dylan nodded.

An emergency room crew met them on the

helipad and helped Casey take Jack's wife straight to the operating room while Dylan transported Jo to the emergency room.

"They've taken Jo for another CT, and then she's going to be admitted to the Neuro Intensive Care Unit. And I'm sure you don't want to hear this, but Alex called and wants us to return to the hospital. One of the electrical linemen fell and needs to be transported to a trauma unit," Dylan said, meeting him at the emergency room entrance.

"This day feels like it will never end," Casey said. He'd managed to grab a sandwich from the break room before they'd left Key West, but eventually he was going to have to stop and sleep. Besides, he didn't want to leave Jo until he made sure she was okay.

"Alex said to let you know that we could bunk at the hospital tonight. Hopefully, this will be our last call for a while," Dylan said.

"Okay, but I need to get the number to where Jo's going to be before we leave."

"I've already got it and sent it to Alex. He's going to call and speak with the neurosurgeon himself, and he said he'd call if there is any change."

Unable to find any other excuse to stay, Casey followed Dylan back to the helipad.

Jo awoke to the sound of monitors beeping and voices outside her room. She'd been woken up every hour during the night for the necessary neuro checks, and she could still feel the effects of the headache she'd had since her fall.

Her hand went to the bandage that covered the stitches on her forehead. The doctor had assured her it would heal with very little scarring. Not that she was worried about the scar. What was one more to add to her collection?

A soft knock came at her door, and a young woman dressed in scrubs, with a badge that read Case Management, walked inside.

"Hi, Ms. Kemp, I'm Cheryl from case management. Do you feel up to talking to me right now? I just have a few questions," the woman carrying a clipboard and pen asked as she stepped up to Jo's bed.

"That's fine. What can I help you with?" Jo could tell the woman was nervous, which didn't make any sense.

"I'm really sorry to disturb you, but the doctor requested that I speak with you about some of the findings on the CTs they performed last night. I understand you fell and injured your head."

Had the CTs last night shown the bleed in her head was expanding? If so, wouldn't it have been the doctor who would have spoken with her about it? "What is this about?"

"I'm sorry. I don't want to upset you, but it seems there were some other injuries, old injuries, that were seen in the X-ray and CTs that were done when you were brought into the hospital. It's our policy to follow up with the patient to make sure that when they are discharged they are going back to a safe environment," the woman explained.

Jo blinked up at her, stunned that she had never thought that her injuries from when she had been abused by Jeffrey would follow her through her medical care.

"It's okay. I'm quite safe to go home. The danger I was in, what caused those injuries, it's in the past."

The woman smiled for the first time since she'd entered the room then looked at her clipboard and jotted something down. "I'm glad to hear that. The only other thing I need to ask is concerning your next of kin. It seems they left that empty when you came in."

Jo started to give the woman's Casey's name then corrected herself, giving the woman her parents' names and number instead. Casey wasn't her next of kin. He wasn't even her real boyfriend. Had she gotten so tied up in this pretend romance that she wasn't sure what was real and what wasn't? Was it possible she'd gotten so tangled up with her own feelings for Casey that she hadn't been able to see that it was all one-sided? That Casey didn't care for her the same way she did for him?

She'd told him that she loved him only for him to try to explain her words away. Was he trying not to hurt her because he didn't return her feelings? It was so easy to see now. The way he kept returning to the fact that all he wanted was friendship, wasn't that what he had done with every other woman she'd seen him date?

She'd been a fool. He'd been trying to let her down easily while she'd continued to insist that there was more between them.

Her cell phone rang, and she looked down to see the picture of Casey on the display.

How could she face him now that she realized she'd been just one more in a line of women who had tried to make Casey love them?

Casey arrived at the hospital and went straight to Jo's room. The last two days had been busy for the Heli-Care crew, with everyone working long shifts helping out the local EMTs as well as helping with transporting patients. The residents had been allowed to return to the Keys, and there had been an increase in the number of accidents as everyone worked to repair their homes. It meant he'd only managed to stop to see Jo once and that was while he was dropping off a patient and she'd been asleep when he'd checked in with her nurse. But today he found her sitting up in the bed, only the bandage on her head hinting that she'd been injured.

"Hey," he said as he walked over to her. He wanted to touch her, to reassure himself that she really was okay. Even though all the reports from the doctors had come back good, he couldn't get that moment when he'd watched her fall out of his mind.

"I didn't expect you," Jo said. "From what

Summer said about the hours you are all having to work, I didn't think I'd see you."

Her words sounded cool and detached, and the smile on her face was a little too bright.

"How are you feeling?" he asked. "Alex said you should be discharged soon."

"I'm discharging today. I'm just waiting for Summer to get here to take me home." Her voice cracked on the last word, and he reached for her hand. Something was wrong. Jo had never acted this way.

"I'll call Summer and let her know I can take you home," he said, pulling out his phone. "If I'd known you were getting out, I would have gotten off sooner."

"Don't," she said as she pulled her hand away from his.

"What's wrong, Jo?"

"I'm not going home with you. All the utilities are back up at my apartment, and Summer is going to pick up Moose for me."

He pulled up one of the chairs and sat. What had changed in the last two days that would cause Jo to not want to return home with him? "I don't understand. Did something happen with Jeffrey?"

"I don't know. I haven't heard from him,

but I don't think he'll turn up in on an island that has just been hit by a hurricane." She took a breath as if gathering her strength then looked him straight in the face. The smile she'd pasted on earlier was gone, and her eyes only held sadness now. "It's time we quit playing this game. I need to go home and get back to my real life and you do too."

"But Jeffrey…" he started.

"If Jeffrey shows up, I'll call the police. I won't let him in the apartment, and I have a lot of neighbors around if I need help. I appreciate everything you did. You've been the best friend I've ever had, but I want to go home now."

The finality of her words and the grave tone of her voice sent a streak of fear down his spine.

"We need to talk about this." He felt like he was poised on a tightrope and one wrong word could bring him crashing down.

"Isn't that my line?" she asked, her lips twitching up. And for the first time since he'd entered the room, he thought he saw a hint of the Jo he knew. "I've had a lot of time to think while I've been in the hospital, and I've decided that you are right. Pretending to be something that we're not isn't good for either of us. It's too easy to get the role-playing confused with reality. It's best that we stop things now."

He wanted to argue with her, but how could he when he'd been the one to blame all the changes in their relationship on their just being confused by the roles they were playing. She'd used his own words against him, and now he had to respect her wishes.

As a nurse walked in and started taking Jo's vital signs, Casey walked out of the room. He knew it was rude to not stay and tell Jo goodbye, but he couldn't bring himself to say the words. Everything about their conversation had seemed so final.

He'd known Jo would return home someday—it had only been a temporary arrangement—but he hadn't known it would hurt like this.

# CHAPTER FIFTEEN

Jo sat in her apartment, Moose draped over her feet, waiting for Summer's reaction. It had been over two weeks since Jo had left the hospital.

"I still can't believe it was all a sham," Summer said, sounding almost as disappointed as Jo. "And you did it all just to keep us away from your ex-husband who should be in jail instead of tormenting you?"

"Don't even think about getting involved. Jeffrey will find a way to hurt you, even if it was just your reputations. He's not worth it. And as far as the courts are concerned, he served the time he was given."

"You underestimate the power of the press. Alex's mother is an expert in controlling the media. She'd send him home looking like the abusive jerk he is," Summer said. "And no matter what you say, I don't believe that you and Casey were faking everything. There was definitely something happening between the two of you the night you babysat for me and Alex. Don't tell me there wasn't."

"Well…" Jo had to tell someone, and since she no longer had a best friend to confide in, Summer was the closest thing she had. The two of them had been close for years. And with Summer's own struggles with an unexpected pregnancy and Alex hiding his life as the son of the king of Soura, she would understand how confusing Jo's life had become.

"We both agreed that we wouldn't let anything come between our friendship. Then there was the night on the beach."

"You mean the one when you kissed Casey like he was one of those juicy Georgia peaches and you were trying to slurp him up? I heard about that. Don't tell me that was faked," Summer said, a smirk on her face as she took a swallow of the fresh lemonade Jo had just made.

"No, I'm not that good an actor." She ignored the flush of heat that traveled down to places better ignored right now as the memory of that night came back.

"So, was it good?" Summer asked, moving closer to the end of her seat.

"Oh, yes," Jo said. "It was very good. At least it was until Casey started acting weird."

"I can't imagine Casey acting weird about sex."

"We didn't have sex, at least not that night. It was the thought of having sex with me. He just doesn't think of me that way." Jo still didn't understand why he saw everything between them as black-and-white. They could be friends but not lovers, yet they'd had a beautiful night together. How did he explain that? Going from friends to lovers had felt natural to her.

"Are you sure? I saw the way he looked at you that night at the house. There was something there. He couldn't take his eyes off you. I would have sworn he was falling in love with you that night."

"One problem with that—Casey doesn't believe in love. He thinks love is just an unnecessary emotion that he can live without." It hurt her to think of him going through the rest of his life never knowing love. Even though he didn't return her love, she'd not been afraid to tell him how she felt. She'd embraced the love she felt for him while he had tossed it back at her. Unwanted. Her love had been unwanted.

"He can't be that stupid. Hasn't he ever been in love?" Summer asked.

"There was a fiancée once. She apparently told him that they'd confused their friendship for love before she broke up with him. He was just using the experience as an excuse to keep all women at a distance."

"I heard something about that. She left the island just before the wedding with someone else. It sounds more like she was trying to excuse her own behavior to me. Surely he's not still hung up on her."

"On her? I don't think so. It's more he blames the situation on what we mortals call love."

They both sat there a moment, each sipping her drink. Men were so hard to understand.

"So you're just going to let him go? If you're in love with him, you should fight for him," Summer said.

"Says the woman who refused to accept that she and the father of her babies could have a future together," Jo said, remembering how heartbroken Summer had been when Alex had left the island without an explanation.

"But Alex didn't give up. Just think what could have happened if he hadn't convinced me that he loved me."

"It's hard to convince someone of something they don't believe in," Jo said.

"Maybe it's not so much that he doesn't believe in it as much as he's afraid of it," Summer said.

Casey afraid of something? It was hard to believe, but Summer could be right. It did seem he ran whenever he heard the word. Could he have been hurt so bad by the things his fiancée had said that he was afraid to trust someone enough to love them?

She shifted on the couch as Moose jumped off her feet and headed to the front door. She stood to follow him even though she wasn't expecting anyone. Her dog was better than any doorbell. Stepping around the big dog who'd planted himself in front of her, she opened the door at the same moment her ex-husband reached for the bell.

She stepped back, putting Moose between them. "What are you doing here, Jeffrey?"

"I came to make sure you're okay, of course.

I was worried about you when that hurricane hit." He flashed her that overly bright smile that she knew was mostly cosmetic. She'd once dreamed of punching every one of those capped teeth out of his mouth. "Aren't you going to let me in?"

She waited for the panic to set in, that heart racing, breath stealing terror that had filled her days and her nights whenever she had thought of this meeting. It didn't come. It was only anger at having her life turned upside down by this man that filled her now.

"I don't think so. You can say whatever it is you came to say right here." What kind of fool did this man think she was? Let him inside her home? No way was that ever happening. Especially not with Summer inside.

As if she knew Jo's thoughts, Summer came up behind her. "Is there a problem?"

"No problem. My ex-husband is just going to explain to me why he felt the need to come visit me when he knew he wouldn't be welcomed." Jo wasn't sure where the courage to stand up to Jeffrey was coming from, but she liked it.

"Is that any way to treat someone who was worried about you? And in front of a royal guest? Princess Summer, I apologize for my wife's bad manners." If the man's smile got any stiffer it would crumble. Jeffrey wouldn't like the fact that Jo was embarrassing him in front of someone as important as Summer. Well, that was too bad. Jo had been preparing for this visit for weeks.

"Summer was just leaving," Jo said as she nodded her head toward the door. Summer didn't need to get involved with any of this.

"Oh, no. I'm not in any hurry. Besides, I want to wait until Casey gets here. He's on his way."

The sickly sweet smile on her ex-husband's face disappeared. "Casey? That guy who had your phone?"

"There's only one Casey. Right, Jo?" Summer's smile was genuine. She'd be a vicious poker player with that smile that gave no hint that she was bluffing. Did she have a plan for what to tell Jeffrey when Casey didn't show up? Or was she just hoping he'd leave before realizing that there was no one coming to their rescue?

But she didn't need Casey to save her. She wouldn't cower in front of this man ever again. He was on her home turf now. She was going to stand her ground. She wasn't the woman he remembered. She'd fight for the life she'd made here in Key West. She would never be that woman again.

"Why did you come here, Jeffrey? Did you think I'd just let you come in and take over my life again? Did you think I'd be too scared to fight you? I'm not that frightened girl anymore."

He started to take a step toward her and then hesitated when Moose let out a low growl of warning. "Don't be so dramatic, Jo. I don't know why you say things like that. There's been a misunderstanding. We need to talk. Alone."

"Dramatic? Me? I'm not the one who put on a show for the lawyers. That was you." She was so tired of reliving that nightmare. "But yes, let's cut the drama. Whatever it is you came for, you're not going to get it. Just leave. Go home. I don't want you here."

"You can't talk to me that way. Who do you think you are? I can make your life miserable, Jo. I came all this way, and you're going to talk to me. Get rid of your friend and this mutt unless you want me to call the police. It wouldn't look very good for your friend when the media hears about her ordering this dog to attack me."

"Don't threaten me," Summer said as she tried to step past Jo.

Tires screeched in the parking lot, and they all watched as Casey rushed out of his truck, heading toward them. What was he doing here?

He'd been on his way to see Jo when he'd received Summer's call. He'd spent the last two weeks alone and miserable, and he was done with it. He'd played over and over in his mind every kiss, every touch he'd shared with Jo in the time they'd been together. And he'd remembered every time he'd denied that there was more than just friendship between them. He'd been so wrong. The weeks they'd shared together hadn't been pretending. They'd shared a home...they'd shared their time together. They'd laughed and danced. And they'd loved together. They'd been happy. Together. He finally understood how the old man with the RV, Jack, had felt. Casey no longer felt whole without Jo beside him.

He wanted to explain all of this to her, but first he had to get rid of her ex-husband.

He'd imagined all kinds of scenarios on his way to Jo's place, each ending with her injured by this dirt bag that once called himself her husband. Now, seeing her safe, he could finally take a deep breath.

"Is there a problem?" Casey asked as he stepped up to the door, pinning Jeffrey between him and Moose. Let the guy try to get around him. He'd been spoiling for this fight ever since he'd seen Jo shake from her fear of this man. Now he just wanted to get rid of this creep so that he could tell Jo he understood. He believed her now. They could be friends and lovers.

"Not anymore," Summer said as she stepped back from the door.

"This man is confused. He seems to think that he can come here, to my home, and threaten me and my friends. He even had some delusional plan to accuse Summer of ordering Moose to attack him," Jo said, her eyes never leaving the man between them.

"Really? And just who are you planning to call? If you need the number to animal control, I have them on speed dial as I volunteer with them at least once a week. Or maybe you'd like to call the local police? They're a great group of guys, though I don't think they're going to believe that bit about Moose since he's pretty well-known around the island as a big old softy."

"This has gone on long enough. I want to talk to my wife. Alone," Jeffrey said. The man's voice never wavered, but Casey could see the bead of sweat that had formed on his forehead, just below that perfect, every-hair-in-its-place haircut.

"That's ex-wife, Jeffrey. And you lost the right to tell me what to do the first time you laid a hand on me. If you came here expecting to find the same woman that you married, you're going to be disappointed. I'm not scared of you anymore. You've done all the damage to me that you could possibly do. I lived. I survived." Jo stepped around Moose and headed forward.

Casey didn't move when the man stepped back. By the time the man's back hit his chest, Casey was smiling with pride. His Jo had the man on the run. "I think it might be best if you leave now. As you can see, there's nothing for you here."

"You think you're something, don't you? You could have come home and lived like a princess. Instead, you'd rather live here in this dump with this mutt, and this…" The man straightened and adjusted the collar of his polo shirt while Casey waited to hear what insult he planned for him. "Well, I hope the two of you live miserably ever after. You deserve it."

Casey stepped back and watched the man as he headed toward the rented sports car sitting in the parking lot. "Well, he told us, didn't he?"

Summer began to laugh until she saw the way Jo had begun to tremble. "Let's get you inside."

"I'm okay. I'm just so mad," Jo said, her hands fisted by her sides.

"We could tell," Summer said. "I was afraid I might have to come up with bail money for you for a moment there."

"It's not Jeffrey I'm mad at. It's me. Why didn't I stand up for myself all those years ago?"

As Moose headed back inside, Casey followed him and Jo before she could come to her senses and slam the door shut in his face.

Summer turned back and studied Casey's expression. When he nodded to the door, she smiled. "If you're okay, I'm going to go. The babies will be waking up from their nap soon."

"You can go too. I don't think he'll come back," Jo said, collapsing onto the couch as Summer left.

"You did good. I was proud of you," he said.

"You're not disappointed that I got all emotional?" she asked, a touch of bitterness in her tone.

"No. I started to get a little emotional myself. I wanted to knock the guy out."

"How did you get here so fast?" she asked.

"I was already on my way here, though I broke all the speed limits once Summer called me."

"You were coming to see me? Why?"

He didn't know how to do this. He was as experienced with women as any man could be, but talking about his feelings? That was hard for him.

"I needed to apologize. I didn't listen when you tried to tell me that there could be something more than friendship between us."

As he talked, he began to walk, the movement calming him as he tried to come up with the perfect words to explain how he felt. "I excused everything that happened between us with the fact that we were pretending to be a couple, when the truth was, we were a couple."

"I don't understand," Jo said, looking up at him.

He stopped pacing and sat down beside her.

"Don't you see? It's always been the two of us. We had this great relationship as friends, but I was always afraid to let there be more. I was always afraid that I'd lose you. That we'd lose the special connection we had. But when we were pretending to be romantically involved, things changed. It gave me the chance to see what it would be like to really be a couple. To share everything. And it felt right. I was just so scared that it wouldn't last, that I denied what we had could be real."

He looked over and saw the confused look on her face. He wasn't doing this right, but all he could do was tell her how he felt. What he now knew was true. "Looking at the two of us, someone would think that I was the strong one because of my size, but that's not true. You stood up to Jeffrey even though you had every right to fear him, while I was too afraid to admit to you, my best friend, that I was in love with you."

"Do you really believe that? That you love me?" Jo asked, her eyes searching his.

"Yes, I know it," Casey said, his eyes never leaving hers. He'd missed this. The way she made him feel complete. He'd never known that was what love felt like.

"Can you say it again?" Jo said, moving closer, taking his face into her hands.

"Of course, I can." He cleared his throat then frowned when Jo laughed. "This is not funny. I'm trying to be serious."

"And I seriously love you, Casey Johnson. See, it's not so hard," Jo said, throwing her arms around him.

"Of course, it isn't. I love you, Jo. See, I can do it. And I don't care what that jerk Jeffrey says. I will never be miserable as long as I have you. You are my happily-ever-after."

# EPILOGUE

GIRLS DREAMED OF fairy-tale endings with their very own Prince Charming while wearing long, white lacey dresses. Once, Jo had given up on those dreams. But now she waited for her turn to walk barefoot down to the sandy shoreline where the man she'd always dreamed of waited for her.

Maybe her Prince Charming was dressed in a white button-up shirt and navy dress pants instead of the standard tux and maybe her dress, though white, didn't have a touch of lace. That was okay. This was her fairy-tale wedding. She could wear whatever she wanted to.

"Are you ready?" Summer asked from beside her.

Jo looked in front of her where a small group of her friends sat in chairs lined up to face the water. She could see her parents among the group. Were they comparing the fancy wedding they'd given her years ago when she'd married Jeffrey to the simple one she and Casey had chosen to have here among their friends? Could they see the love in Casey's eyes when he looked at her instead of the possessiveness that had always been in Jeffrey's?

"Okay, Violet," Summer said as she motioned for Dylan's daughter to walk down the deep blue runner that ran down to the beach where Casey waited.

Summer squeezed Jo's hand before turning and following the little girl. Then it was Jo's turn. She took her first step, and Moose bumped against her side.

"You're doing fine," she told him, giving his head a rub. He was taking his job of escorting her down the aisle very seriously.

Reaching Casey's side, she turned to see her friends and family gathered behind her as he took her hand and they stepped forward to commit their lives to each other while the sun began to set behind them.

Later, when the toasts had been made and the DJ took requests, Jo wandered down to the beach alone. Laughter drifted down from the pavilion where everyone was dancing, but she could still hear the soft footsteps behind her.

"Are you already trying to sneak away from me?" Casey said as his arms came around her waist.

"Or maybe I'm trying to sneak away with you," she said, leaning back against him.

"I like the sound of that. Happy?" he asked as his lips skimmed down her throat.

"I've never been happier," she said, turning around in his arms. "I have you, my friends and this beautiful island. I think I might have the very best happily-ever-after a girl could ever dream of."

\* \* \* \* \*

*If you enjoyed this story, check out these other great reads from Deanne Anders*

Pregnant with the Secret Prince's Babies
Florida Fling with the Single Dad
December Reunion in Central Park
The Neurosurgeon's Unexpected Family

*All available now!*